Helen Alice Nitsch

Molly Bishop's family by Helen Alice Nitsch

Helen Alice Nitsch

Molly Bishop's family by Helen Alice Nitsch

ISBN/EAN: 9783743337602

Manufactured in Europe, USA, Canada, Australia, Japa

Cover: Foto ©Andreas Hilbeck / pixelio.de

Manufactured and distributed by brebook publishing software
(www.brebook.com)

Helen Alice Nitsch

Molly Bishop's family by Helen Alice Nitsch

MOLLY BISHOP'S FAMILY

BY

CATHERINE OWEN

AUTHOR OF " TEN DOLLARS ENOUGH," AND "GENTLE BREADWINNERS "

BOSTON AND NEW YORK
HOUGHTON, MIFFLIN AND COMPANY
The Riverside Press, Cambridge
1888

The Riverside Press, Cambridge:
Electrotyped and Printed by H. O. Houghton & Co.

PREFATORY NOTE.

THE author wishes to state that, in the narrative of Mrs. Bishop's bringing up of her children, she does not write from theory, but from experience, not only her own, but the far wider and less personal experience gained from attentive observation of that of others. She deprecates all wish to dogmatize, or to impose her views on her readers; she would not even recommend their adoption, where they involve questions of diet and health, without the sanction of the family physician, because, although not one child, but several, furnish the data from which her conclusions are drawn, it is nevertheless true, constitutions differ so widely that, although ninety children out of a hundred will thrive under certain conditions, the other ten may require entirely different ones. It is the author's firm belief that a *healthy well* infant will be also a contented and good one, *if* it has fair play ; but while the mother is still helpless, it too often acquires habits which make the first three months of its life a torment to the house. The exceptions to this rule may generally be traced to the ante-natal mental condition of the mother.

The author does not pretend to do more than offer her experience, and that of some other mothers, to those who may be looking forward to maternity and desire to inform themselves ; the already experienced matron will very naturally either agree or not agree, as her own observation may lead her.

CONTENTS.

MOLLY BISHOP'S FAMILY.

CHAPTER I.

SOMETHING ABOUT THE BABY.

"MRS. BISHOP, if your child is healthy and you are as wise as I think, you will have little trouble with a crying baby; but remember, a baby's digestion has everything to do with its health, and that, in nine cases out of ten, is ruined in *the first month* of its life."

"But how can I guard against it, doctor?" Mrs. Bishop had asked.

"More depends on the nurse than on you; but if she is a sensible woman you will be all right, and if she is not, nothing you can do will have any other effect than to worry you, and upset the child."

"Oh, doctor, let me be sure and have a sensible nurse. I had hoped to have one who has been with Mrs. Lennox, but I'll leave it to you."

"If you have her, she will suit you. She will not allow the baby to be overfed, nor will she destroy its stomach with teas and doses. Depend upon it, the more a baby is left to nature the better it will be. Nature does n't need half so much assistance as people think."

And Mrs. Lennox, whose children had charmed her, had said almost the same.

"I don't believe young babies ever cry from temper. If they cry they are uncomfortable, but it does n't follow that the discomfort comes from hunger, as most people seem to think; it quite as often comes from an over-full stomach. Yet your nurse will, most likely, tell you it needs feeding, and if its last food has not digested, it is given more to increase its trouble. Only one of my babies was cross. It was the first. I had no experience, my nurse believed in anise-seed and catnip tea, and during the first month, if it cried after nursing, it was declared to have colic, and a spoonful of anise-seed tea or catnip was given. It was walked about, and patted and jumped, and in an hour if it cried again it was hungry, and had to be nursed; but I think for the first six weeks it never passed an hour without crying; then I came to Greenfield, and old Dr. Price came to attend the baby for an attack of some sort of fever, and I asked him if it was a healthy child. He told me it was perfectly so, and I then told him that it was fretful. He asked some questions, and said:

" 'It is only the old story : the baby has n't fair play. Don't you know the stomach of a baby is n't much larger than an egg? and yet you let it take food every time it cries, and when it is uncomfortably full, you give it sickening teas. Now, if you are sensible, you 'll drop the teas, and feed it only at stated intervals; every two and a half hours is often enough for a healthy child who can take a hearty meal, and when three months old it will need food only once in three hours. A weak child can take very little food at a time, and requires more frequent feeding.'

" But if it cries for food " —

" 'Oh, it will cry because you have fed it every time it did cry. It does n't want the food, but it likes the warmth and cuddling up ; but had n't you better let it cry till it gets used to the new regimen, than to have it constantly fretting? It will only be for a few days.'

" I followed his advice, for I had tried the old way and found the baby was unhappy, and I was worn out. I fed it only at stated times, and for the first week I had a terrible struggle; then gradually the change came, baby was content, it slept as well again, and rarely fretted; if it had a real hard crying spell now, I knew that it meant pain. At such times I undressed and put it in a warm blanket near the fire and rubbed the little limbs with my warm hand. Generally the undressing was enough, but in case it was not, I put it in a warm bath, still by Dr. Price's orders. 'There are little aches and pains of which we can know nothing,' he had said; 'they may be from the prick of a pin, or they may be colic, and there are other little pains to which babies are subject, for all of which a warm bath is certain relief.'"

Mrs. Bishop's friends and neighbors were deeply interested in seeing how she would manage with a baby. There were many predictions that her theories would all go to the winds when the baby arrived, just as Mrs. Somebody else's music had been given up and Mrs. Other one's painting. The peculiarity was, that Mrs. Bishop's hobby, which it was expected would become an unused steed, was so prosaic a matter as one branch of housekeeping — cooking; and at the first glance it would seem odd that the arrival of a baby, one of the household, should be expected to change its mother's views; other women did not keep house less well after the first baby came. The explanation was this: —

Mrs. Bishop had elected, when she began to keep house, to give her chief attention to the cooking; all other work she could pay some one to do; that work she could not get done for any reasonable amount to suit her, and therefore, although her husband had only an average clerk's salary, her table had been as dainty as if they had employed a professional cook.

When I say she gave her attention chiefly to cooking, I must be understood as speaking comparatively. Whatever pressure there was on her time, it did not occur to her that the dinner could be less well served, although the parlor sweeping might be put off. But although, to Mrs. Bishop, the kitchen was the heart of the house, I do not mean to say that the other part was neglected; it was very well kept by her servant; I think, perhaps, there were fewer of the charming coquetries women love in their rooms than in some others, and the pretty trifles there were — for the house was by no means destitute of pretty things — were not such as bore testimony to its mistress's nimble needle, but were rather the flotsam gathered during some years of foreign residence.

She had sometimes lamented, since her marriage, that she had not persevered in doing fancy work when she saw the lovely work of other women, until she reflected that it was less trouble to her to make herself a charming dress than it would be to make a South Kensington tidy, and that she could buy the tidy far better made for less money than the dressmaker's bill would come to; but she had a thrifty soul and did not buy it, so her rooms were devoid of tidies.

She was not proud of the deficiency, nor did she despise pretty handiwork; indeed, she had more than once wished it would occur to her friends that she was fond of it, and that they would make her the offering of their fingers, instead of some other things; but when she began to keep house, or rather before she began to do so, she had thought over the matter of her duties very seriously. Her husband's means had been small, his tastes and her own somewhat luxurious, and she had but one pair of hands; they would keep one maid, but Molly (Mrs. Bishop was always called Molly by her friends) well knew that even a small house cannot be kept in perfect order by one servant without a good deal of assistance from the mistress, unless the table is made a very secondary matter, and she chose to do what another could not do so well. This was the difference between her housekeeping and that of some others. She knew that many housekeepers scrimped the time from the kitchen in order to do what seemed more important work for the house.

Molly had passed her girlhood in France and England with a very careful and sensible mother, an invalid, and there she had imbibed the habit of thinking the preparation of the meals the most important, at all events the least to be neglected, part of housekeeping. Her mother had always declared that the reason why dyspepsia was hardly ever known in France and Germany was because so much more attention was paid to cooking by the housewives in those countries than in her own. This conviction, right or wrong, had sunk into the girl's mind, as mother's words always do, and when she came back to America she had noticed that if a housekeeper was hurried, it was the table that suffered. This, once in a way, would not have mattered, but the majority were always hurried, and some with whom she had talked had told her frankly, that they always got for dinner whatever was most easily and quickly cooked. When *young* wives had said this, she had ventured to question the wisdom, but was quickly silenced, but not convinced, by one declaring that she did not make a god of her stomach, that her husband preferred her to devote herself to study, so as to be his intellectual companion. Another said, "Neither she nor her husband cared for the pleasures of the table, — they ate to live, and did not live to eat;" and others protested their husbands' supreme contentment with old-fashioned simplicity, which meant, she found invariably, the easiest cooked and the longest lasting food. What struck Molly most was the fact that the ladies who had pleaded intellectual reasons were very mediocre young women; had they possessed a single talent, she could have understood the reasoning, for, assuredly, a gift is too precious a thing to be neglected, but the one or two most gifted women she knew, strange to say, seemed to nurse their intellect very little, and to forget they had a mind if the family comfort made calls on their hands.

"And the worst of it is," she had written to her friend, Mrs. Welles, "they don't seem to see that it is not only a matter of enjoyment or non-enjoyment of one's food, but that it actually means health!"

No, Molly found bad plumbing, ill ventilated rooms, malarious situations, were all discussed and battled with, by the very people who could not perceive that heavy bread, poor butter, tough meat, and ill-cooked vegetables had as much influence on the health as any, or all of these ; for what a man eats is his life, just as much as the air he breathes, so much so that physicians tell us an *entire* change of diet, say from mixed food to milk or grapes, for three months, will entirely change our blood.

But then, these good ladies who had souls above kitchen work had not attended the South Kensington Lectures on Food, and Molly had.

When Molly began housekeeping herself, she resolved that whatever was neglected in her house, it must never be the kitchen work. If necessary, the parlor could be shut up, and the dining-room do double duty, the spare chamber be given over to dust and moths, but her dinner table must not suffer. Aside from the coarseness of eating ill-cooked food, there was the question of health. The one ailment she dreaded for husband or possible children was dyspepsia, the destroyer, not of life, but of all the enjoyment of life. No! rather than that spectre should sit at her banquets, she would dress like a Quakeress and work like a beaver.

The parlor had not been sacrificed, nor did dust and moths invade her spare chambers; for Molly had found a fairly good servant in a green German girl named Marta, who brought, with utter ignorance, a strong pair of hands and a willing heart, but no mind to speak of; and during the few months that Mrs. Bishop kept house before her baby was born, she had faithfully lived up to her resolution. Many of those who had watched her had said, " Wait till the baby comes; that will make sad havoc with your fancy cooking, my dear. You will be glad then to get a bit of roast beef on the table that will last a couple of days, and order a pie from the bakery like the rest of us."

Now, although Mistress Molly had smiled, and said no doubt the baby would occupy much of her time, she had also taken another resolution, and that was to learn all she could about babies, and

whether it might not lie largely with herself if
it should take all her time, or not more of it
than she could spare.   She read, and inquired,
and talked to the old physician who gave her
the foregoing advice. This was supplemented by
Mrs. Lennox's experience. The children of this
friend had always been a wonder and admiration
to Mrs. Bishop; they seemed to her to combine
all that is most charming in childhood; they were
gay and frolicsome, apparently unrestrained by
any fear of offending their parents, yet never
causing a visitor to feel that they required re-
buke. We all know how irritating other people's
children often are, how we feel we really would
not allow this or that, — the teasing to have their
own way when it would be bad for them, the
squabbling and unwilling obedience to parental
requirements that too often make one feel
acutely for the mother's weariness; but with the
Lennox children there was none of this. Little
rows among themselves they did have occasionally, for they were not angelic, but their mother
was never teased, they never caused one to think
her weakly indulgent, and yet no more tender
mother could be imagined. Mrs. Bishop watched
and studied this family, for she could not understand at first whether the children were of unusually fine tempers, or whether Mrs. Lennox,
simple-natured and excellent as she was, had

strength of character enough to have brought this about by scarcely felt discipline. She found later that this quiet, gentle lady was as softly persevering as the flower that by its silent pressure uplifts the stone in its way. The children yielded to the quiet influence that encompassed them, unconscious of restraint because they had great latitude in unimportant matters; on all important ones it never occurred to them to dispute the mother's rule. But although she had conscientiously taken note of all these things, storing them up to aid her own inexperience, she found after the baby was born that she had to fight for her own way with it. Her husband's mother had brought up a large family, and clung to the old ways. The idea of stinting a baby in its food was an enormity, only possible to a "theorist," as she was fond of calling her daughter - in - law. Then when Molly insisted that it should have no soothing teas if it cried, and not be rocked to sleep, Mrs. Bishop senior lost patience, and prophesied terrible things. They did not come to pass, but that, she declared, was owing to the child's wonderful constitution inherited from its father.

CHAPTER II.

"SPARTAN MOTHERS."

BEFORE the baby was born, Molly had been careful to teach Marta how to prepare certain meals all through without referring to her. She had then written out seven bills of fare, one for each day, comprising breakfast and dinner, with light luncheon for any one who might be there. She did not want the predicted decadence in her table to begin for her husband directly she was out of the way.

She laughingly told him that he must not dare to have any caprices, for Marta was wound up to cook each dinner just as written.

"If you suggest an alteration it will upset the whole thing. If you want to have Tuesday's soup on Wednesday, that will bewilder her and the dinner go all wrong."

"Never mind if it does, Molly. It would n't hurt me to go without a dinner once in a while, or I can get it in town."

"Oh, I shall not worry about it. I spoke more for Marta's sake than yours. No, don't get dinner in town, because there will be no occasion for that, and beside it would be bad for Marta and take away her sense of responsibility. She knows she must rely on herself. To assume that she can't do so, before we try her, will be needless."

"Anything you like, Molly."

When the time drew near for the nurse to leave, Molly began to bathe the baby herself. She had had a bath made by the carpenter, which stood on two cross legs (about the height of her knees), and a piece of rubber sheeting was nailed over the top with enough "bag" in the middle to hold the water. When not in use it was folded and put away. In this soft, yielding bath no unexpected movement of the child could hurt its tender flesh.

The first bath Molly gave with fear and trembling, the flesh seemed so tender, the little bones so soft, and the baby cried. Certainly, it cried lustily. It is true it had always cried with the nurse, so she could not be hurting it. Her arm and hand were under the little head and body to support it while she washed with softest sponge. Nevertheless, she was thankful to lift it on to her flannel-covered knees (she wore a large apron of thick, soft flannel), and wipe it dry with soft, old damask towels. How nervous she was for fear she might not dry every crevice

and fold, and yet afraid of hurting it by too
much drying.   "Oh, if it would not cry so!
I've heard of babies enjoying the bath," said
Molly, looking flushed and rather tired when the
last garment was on, and the little pink bundle
in its warm wrapper was reaching out for food.

"Yes, ma'am; but most young babies make a
rumpus.   She'll enjoy it when she's a little
older; but a little crying won't hurt her, — it's
about all the crying she does in the twenty-four
hours."

This was true, whether due to Molly's training,
or, as its grandmother said, to its father's angelic
nature and good constitution, I will not pretend
to say, but the baby was remarkably good.   It
slept the better part of the day and all night.
This last was so unlike the traditional baby that
Harry had asked with a smile, that, however, did
not conceal real anxiety, "This baby of yours,
Molly, is such an outrageous sleeper!   You don't
think, do you, that Mrs. Watts doses it slyly?"

"Harry," cried Molly, in horror, "I should
go wild if I thought so!   Oh, no; the doctor and
Mrs. Lennox vouch for her, and the doctor says
it's exactly what is natural for a baby to do —
to eat and sleep."

"There are very few natural babies, then, I'm
afraid."

But the young father was very proud of having

one so unlike the majority, and boasted loudly that he had not once been wakened by it, nor did he mind when some laughed and whispered, " Poppies."

When Molly had nursed the baby she laid it down to go to sleep. A " Spartan mother," the grandmother had called her, in wrathful ridicule, when first she saw the few hours' old baby laid down in its blanket to sleep. But though her words had been meant to sting, they were true in a way she did not guess. To her, and others, who cling to the rocking and walking of babies to sleep, the reverse method means selfish rest and self-indulgence at baby's expense. They think — perhaps they reach the conclusion without thinking — that the mother refuses to put her baby to sleep in her arms because she prefers to do something else. The mother thus gets rid of the baby as much as possible. They do not for a moment realize that it requires Spartan self-denial to choose this part; that it would be far more sweet to indulge the mother weakness which yearned to have that tender little baby in her arms always; that no luxury could be greater than to sit by the hour, hushing and cuddling it, and dreaming over it, watching even its finger nails grow. Nor could they guess that every cry which she thinks she could still with love and caresses goes like a knife to the mother heart.

Molly at least had to use resolute self-control and to remember that her own pleasure was bad for her child, to prevent her herself from giving all her time to it. So far as her own enjoyment went, it would have slept till it woke again in her arms. Not to sleep with it close to her bosom was to give up a great luxury, for it seemed part of herself. She lacked something of herself when it was not near her. Yet, she knew if she indulged her own yearnings she would probably have a fretful, wailing child. Although she smiled at her mother-in-law's railing, she thought, with tears in her eyes, how true it was that Spartan courage indeed was required not to let the tiny new-comer become the one absorbing sweetness of her life.

" It requires far more love to be firm than to be indulgent," she thought.

There was another point in her baby's up-bringing that she had heard her mother descant upon, and which she decided for herself, and that was that there should be no unusual silence while baby slept. She had no whispering or tiptoeing round the house. If the nurse or her husband spoke, it was in the natural voice, even in the same room; but of course all violent or sudden noises were avoided.

Her mother had often spoken of how she had accustomed Molly herself to sleep through all

the every-day sounds, and how her sister's child
was put to sleep in a dark room, the whole
household silenced, — its father not daring to
rattle the pages of a newspaper, and every one
forced to creep about for a certain time during
the day, with the result that every trivial out-
door sound beyond control, an accidental word
uttered in the natural key, sufficed to wake it.

This again was a subject of contention between Molly and her mother-in-law. "You 'll
ruin that child's nerves, Molly," she said, when
Molly explained why she did not whisper her
greeting at the door of the room in which it
slept. She insisted on whispering herself then
and always, if the baby was asleep.

"I hope not. I 'm afraid you think I am very
obstinate, and that I am victimizing our darling
to my ignorant theories; and I know you are
almost as fond of her as I am, so I want you to
be easy on the subject. I am not alone in these
'new-fangled notions.' Doctors who devote
their lives to the treatment of children, ladies
who have spent the greater part of their time in
institutions for them, all testify to the need of
regularity and "—

"Molly! do you compare *my* grandchild to
those brought up in institutions?" cried the
lady, deeply offended. "Don't we all pity
those poor little souls! Are you satisfied to give

your child no more affection than those little heart-starved things?"

Tears were actually in her worldly eyes as she spoke, and Molly, while she despaired of convincing her, forgave her prejudice for the sake of those tears.

"I only wanted to assure you that I am not heedlessly trusting to my own ideas. I have talked to Dr. Price, and you can't suppose I don't love my baby far too well to risk a mistake," she added, indignantly.

"You are so set, my dear; although it is not you alone I blame, but all the new ideas, — as if the world had n't gone on and babies been born and lived and thrived for thousands of years, as nature, not books, dictates."

CHAPTER III.

CHOOSING FURNITURE.

I WONDER if there is a much more enjoyable time in a woman's life than when she sees herself about to enter a house exactly to her taste, and has the money to furnish it; a limited amount, perhaps, but the pleasure of making it go as far as it will is all the greater. The pleasure may be sadly marred by circumstances which to the mind of the practical might seem advantageous, if you have had the misfortune to have inherited furniture, good, solid, and ugly, which yet your thrifty soul will not let you discard; or, worse still, have been presented at your wedding with ornaments and pictures that make you shudder, and yet which you will be forced to place prominently for fear of wounding some dear artless giver. Mrs. Bishop had nothing of this kind to interfere with her pleasure, and a few things to enhance it, for she had a loving husband who had " builded better than he knew " when he married her, and was now, after three years, only beginning to find it out, — at least so he said, — and what could add more to a wife's happiness than such saying, after three years! And now she was going to furnish a charming little house; not at all a costly one, but built as she would have wished had it been done to her order. It was just large enough, had a well planned kitchen, a spacious piazza, a garden, and was prettily decorated inside.

She had been contemplating her bliss for nearly three months, and now she was strong again, the baby well, the spring just at hand, and the country just at the least pleasant season. So at the end of March it was decided to spend a month in New York for the delightful purpose of shopping leisurely. Mr. and Mrs. Bishop senior had a very fine house near the park, and were anxious to receive their son and his wife, but more especially the baby.

"I am sorry if your father will be disappointed, Harry; but it will be much better to board."

"He will be disappointed, Molly, — no doubt about that."

"Then let us give up the idea, for you know as well as I do that your mother and I differ about baby, and a month of struggle to have my own way, or else a month of changed habits for the child, which will alter its disposition altogether, I cannot stand. It would be lovely to be in New

York, to be able to look for the very things we want and not buy till we find them, but other people manage very well by only going in a day at a time ; so will we."

"Oh, no, that won't do. Molly, you shall do as you like ; the struggle will have to come, and may as well soon as late."

" Perhaps not. It is quite true that to live in the sixties, when I want to shop down town, with a baby needing me every three hours, will be very inconvenient. Then dear Charlotte, who lives in such a central spot, we have refused ; so, if you make the very most of that, perhaps your mother may not feel angry, and once we have made our purchases we can spend a few days with her."

" Very well ; I 'll see about board to-day, then."

And so it came about that, although Mr. and Mrs. Bishop's parents had so large a house, the young couple installed themselves in a modest boarding-house near Washington Square, where they had lived the first year of their married life.

Perhaps some of my readers may think that Mrs. Bishop was rather a remarkable young woman, but I assure you she did not think so herself, which makes the offense — if any would find fault ; and she would have shuddered had any one hinted, which no one who knew her (not even her mother-in-law) ever did, that she was

" strong-minded." If I were asked to charac-
terize her I should say, if women like her were
more frequently found, that she was the legitimate result of a nineteenth-century (the latter
half of it) education. Without being specially
gifted, she was sagacious, acute, and an embodi-
ment of common sense ; and yet not quite the
prosaic little body such qualities might indicate,
for she had a dash of romance or sentiment or
poetry, or what you will, about her that softened
what might have been otherwise a rather too decided character. But although common sense
was her chief gift, she had found herself so con-
spicuous among the coterie in which she lived by
reason of it that it required rather a vigorous
appeal to that gift to prevent her believing herself a genius. She was now in danger of thinking, not that *she* was above what the average
woman should be, but that the majority were
below it.

But although her married life had not been
one of great ease or great prosperity, it had so
far been entirely happy, and since the new house
had been taken, and especially since the dear
baby had come, her cup seemed brimming over.
Sometimes she would sigh with utter content as
she realized that she had every wish gratified.

Her dearest friend, Mrs. Welles, although a
very happy woman herself, yet could hardly
understand Molly's joyful content.

" You must be very much in love with Harry,
Molly," she said one day when the latter had
said, rather solemnly, "I am almost frightened
at having every wish fulfilled; it cannot last."

Mrs. Welles laughed. "Don't let that fear be
your one crumpled rose-leaf. It's your own nature that makes your happiness. I know a dozen
women who could put a 'but' in it. Harry is a
dear good fellow, but not better than most men
I know. Don't you think Mrs. A. and Mrs. D.
have everything you have and rather more? but
have they such an oppressive sense of their blessings, do you think? Was n't Mrs. A. worrying
because her sealskin was shabby and Mr. A.
could not spare money for a new one? And
was n't Mrs. D. full of weariness because she has
only one servant, and has to be 'mistress and
maid too,' as she characterized it?"

"Yes, I know, and wonder sometimes how
they let such little miseries worry them; but I
am also conscious that I have a tremendous
capacity myself for being unhappy about things
that would not trouble many. Just imagine if
any one dear to me or Harry had given us such
a proof of loving industry as Mr. Framley's
mother gave them, — a plaster Venus di Medici
colored by herself, with blue eyes, golden hair,
and tinted skin, and then expect it to be of
course the leading ornament of the drawing-
room!"

" Molly, you don't mean it ! "

" I do. I never have liked Mrs. Framley much, but since I saw that, and saw her painful flush when she explained that it was her mother-in-law's work, I have respected her very much. I 'm afraid a very bad picture would be capable of making me miserable if I were forced to have it before my eyes, or else wound some one's feelings. And that is what makes me so determined to think well, and not to buy one single ugly thing, or one that we may tire of."

"That is right; think what a nightmare of ugliness we were all brought up in ! "

Molly had written down a list of the articles they would need, and hoped to get every essential for a thousand dollars. A few months before she would have said five hundred, and would have said she could furnish neatly and prettily. Now there was no need for such a low limit; but even now she knew she must watch all the small expenditures very closely in order not to fritter the money away. Trifles that cost " only a dollar," or " only five," are the little foxes that eat into large sums, which melt like snow in the sun. She had drawn up a list of articles they actually must have, and resolved not to be tempted to make a single purchase outside of them until they were all bought.

This was all the harder to accomplish, perhaps,

since her husband did not second her in this economy. His position was improved, he was junior partner in his father's business, and could not see, as he had three thousand dollars in the bank, why she should not spend double on the house, if she wished.

"For one thing, because I think it will be more in keeping with the character of the house to be prettily rather than handsomely furnished; and then we never know what may happen. When Meg (the baby's name was Margaret) grows up we may like a larger house. By that time our furniture will have done its duty, if we do not pay too much, and we can refurnish. The money we save can go towards it."

"Well, don't get bureau-drawers that make a man want to swear every time he goes for a clean shirt; nor get cadaverous glasses, nor weak-kneed chairs."

"All those things I will religiously avoid, in fact have pledged myself to do so. I forego style."

"Although a woman!"

"Although a woman. Style and solidity do not go together under a certain large number of dollars. I seek beautiful simplicity and strength at as low a price as may be."

"May I be there to see when you 've found them?"

"You will, dear; I shall buy nothing until you have approved."

Molly had already seen bedroom furniture at a warehouse several months before that had fulfilled her ideal. It was called Eastlake, and was made with the severest simplicity. The simple lines were without any ornament, — not a scroll or button. Four lines of grooving ran up the posts. Other lines surrounded the head and footboard, and framed the glass which was large and square. The wood was ash, and not a cent had been wasted on ornament. But although the furniture was as low in price as such well-made work could be, she had not been sure when she saw it that she might not have to content herself with painted pine.

To this store she went and found that there was nothing of the kind there now; she tried many others. Everywhere she found bedroom sets at lower prices even for ash, but how sadly cheap they looked! Everywhere she went, cheap ornament and poor workmanship, or else high prices and still, ornament.

At last she went back to the store where she had seen the Eastlake sets.

"Is n't it possible that I can get furniture exactly like what I saw here five months ago?"

"Oh, yes; we can order it again, if you will point out the style in this book."

Molly quickly did so, found that she had to pay something more than the price she had then been asked, but gladly did it. She ordered two sets, and one of painted pine for the servants' room.

In talking over the parlor furniture, Harry and herself had agreed not to have any expensive stuffed chairs, but three or four rattan easy-chairs, the most comfortable to be found.

"Don't buy a chair that isn't comfortable to sit in, Molly. I hate those stereotyped parlor chairs that you try to keep every one from sitting in, because you know they are uncomfortable. What is the sense of having a chair in the room of which you are obliged to say, 'Oh, don't sit in that, this is much more comfortable'?"

"I agree with you. And there are such dear little gossip chairs now."

So the rattan armchairs, stained of a rich warm tan (which Molly saw in her mind's eye invested with downy cushions of peacock-blue), with three quaint but very cosy little gossip chairs, and a rocker of the kind that is very comfortable but takes little room, and whose tall, straight back of twisted cherry has a certain dignity not belonging to rockers, comprised the sitting accommodation of the parlor. These all cost less than the usual half a dozen stuffed

chairs would have done if well made, even without covering ; but they had decided that the one
extravagance must be a broad, low, Turkish
lounge.   When of good quality, these are never
low-priced, but they are the only really comfortable kind of lounge.   This was bought uncovered, and a lounge rug of oriental color and
fabric (so called) was bought to cover it.   It
cost less than covering of equally good quality.

For the parlor rug, a very deep Indian blue
was chosen, with an almost invisible pattern of
a blue that was almost black.   For this also she
hunted through many stores.   She had of course
no special pattern in mind ; but a dark, oriental
blue carpet without pattern, or so small a one
that the general effect should still be blue, was
what she wanted.   Of course, as she was limited
to a hundred dollars for a fourteen-feet-square
rug, she could only buy a soft, thick, Wilton
carpet and have it made.   This was excellent of
its kind and better than a cheap oriental rug.

For the dining-room and bedrooms, however,
she bought Japanese rugs.   Those for the bedrooms were exceedingly pretty, in willow-blue
shades, and being all cotton they were moth-
proof.

CHAPTER IV.

WHAT TO DO?

"I AM getting very anxious about Mary. She is sixteen, and I cannot see that she has any special talent for anything; yet of course she must earn her own living."

The speaker was Mrs. Lennox, and Mary was her eldest girl. She had often, during the last few months, spoken of her anxiety as to her daughter's future to Molly, and then the matter had dropped.

"I know you must be anxious. What does Mary say?"

"Well, she does *not* say, that is the worst of it. But she will docilely take up any course I decide upon."

Molly, without any special reason, had watched the girl, and had seen that, although she was bright, she was not adapted to teaching; indeed, Mrs. Lennox had wisely decided not to prepare her for that overcrowded profession to which every young girl of a certain social class seemed to turn. She had not her mother's love of sewing, but was quite able to turn her hand to all useful things.

"You know it is my firm conviction that if a woman does any one thing thoroughly well, she can make a living; even in teaching, over-crowded as that profession is, any one who is more thorough than the average will never need employment, although I agree with you that it is the last thing to choose. It is so much easier when a girl or boy shows some decided leaning toward one thing. I can't understand people thwarting their wishes; they might be sure they would not succeed so well in other things."

At this point Mrs. Welles, Mrs. Bishop's intimate friend, who was living near her, came in. Meg, who was now toddling about and making bold efforts to climb up stairs and probably to fall down, which it took considerable vigilance to frustrate, greeted her with a scream and out-stretched arms, and was seized and hugged to her heart's content, for Mrs. Welles was Meg's chief idolater.

"We were talking, Charlotte, about Mary Lennox and what she is to do in life. Women's work is rather a hobby of yours, can you help us?" asked Molly, as she made room for her friend on the piazza.

"I don't suppose so. My hobby, as you call

it, is only on one phase of woman's work. I
don't think it is so necessary to find new em-
ployments for women, although that would be a
good thing, as to teach that women must do
thoroughly the work ready to their hands. Only
this morning I read in a London paper that
there are hundreds of seamstresses requiring
work, and quite as large a number of ladies who
say they cannot get work fairly well done except
at higher prices than they can afford, which
means that average seamstresses do not sew well
enough to obtain employment, and that those
who work better than the average have more
than they can do, and so charge very high
prices. If this is true of a crowded city like
London, it is even more true here. If we want
a gown made we can get it by going to a first-
rate dressmaker and paying a first-rate price;
but one does not want to buy a charming sateen
at twenty-five cents a yard and pay even ten
dollars to get it made. A seamstress will make
it for three, but unless one is quite unable to
cut, we know our own fit and taste will be so
much better that we do it ourselves. I have
never learned dressmaking nor have a special
talent for it, yet, if I want a dress made over, I
can do it myself so that it will look graceful and
not clumsy. If I plan it and fix it and give it
out to a seamstress, it may possibly give me some

pleasure, but I have used time that I needed
for other matters, and, besides, if I must plan,
I would as soon do the whole thing; so you see
she goes without the work, and I keep money in
my pocket I would rather have paid out. Only
this morning I heard of a woman needing work;
I inquire, and am told her intentions are good,
she is industrious, but she cannot be trusted
with work requiring care."

"I can tell you of a woman, Charlotte; she
really can plan and alter just as one would one's
self. She is a woman named Gibbs."

"I am so glad to know of her, but I must
make haste and avail myself, for I am quite sure
she will not be long without work."

"Oh, I don't mean that she is, she has a
great deal more than she can do; only if you
want work done and speak a week or two ahead,
you need have no planning."

"Now, is n't that exactly what I have said?"
cried Mrs. Welles, triumphantly. "There are
several industrious women here needing work,
but this one, who does unusually well, has more
than she can do; and, after all, it is often not
skill or training in a sewing-woman that is
needed, only care and observation, with the ambition to do, not 'well enough,' but as well as
possible."

Mrs. Welles's gray eyes were luminous with

her earnestness. Molly smiled demurely and
then said :

" Well, what shall Mary Lennox learn thoroughly ? Her mother will see that she understands that gospel well."

" Oh, her mother must be a much better
judge. What does she like ? "

" Nothing, especially, but gardening, nor does
she dislike anything ; I wish she did, it would
at least be something to avoid."

" Then why not gardening ? "

" Gardening ! " cried Mrs. Lennox, while
Molly looked wonderingly at her friend.

" Yes. Don't you think florists get rich ? Is
there a place in Greenfield where you can buy a
bunch of roses if you want ? And didn't you,
Molly, write to me Easter to get you a few
lilies ? And only last week I saw Mr. Framley
carrying home a box of cut flowers."

" Oh, yes ; if we want anything but carna-
tions, geraniums, heliotropes, and smilax, in winter, we have to send to New York. Our solitary florist never has more than one rose at a
time in bloom, and rarely that," said Molly.

Mrs. Lennox looked thoughtful.

" It is certainly worth thinking about."

Mrs. Welles was at once interested.

" You will be a sensible mother if you let
Mary make an effort in the direction in which

her taste really lies; but do not let her be satisfied with growing just what every small florist
has. She must make the subject, or, better still,
some one branch of it, her study; read up every
good authority, and experiment for the next four
years; and, trust me, when she is twenty, she
will be able to take care of herself. And if
she has real taste and enthusiasm, she will do
more; for instance, if she produces finer flowers than the average, she will soon become
widely known. It is remaining at the dead
level average, and being satisfied with that, that
is fatal to prosperity."

"I think, in cultivating flowers, Mary will
not rest until she produces the very best of the
kind she has ever seen. Her pansies we are all
proud of, and she read in a newspaper, last year,
how to have pond-lilies without a pond, and has
been so anxious to try. But you know we have
very little money to indulge our tastes, so, small
as the cost might be, she cannot indulge herself.
However, if it is to help her in future, the
money should not be lacking."

"Pansies are always in such demand, why not
make a specialty of them if your ground is
suited? I always recommend a specialty, by
which I mean directing all one's efforts to doing
one thing especially well, rather than dividing
one's efforts up among many things; and it is

the one superior thing that people run after and pay great prices for, rather than the average one they can buy on every block."

"Hear, hear," said Molly, clapping her hands gently; and little Meg, who had been sitting on a mat between the three, apparently engaged in discovering the inner mechanism of a woolen lamb, dropped it suddenly and clapped her chubby hands in imitation of her mother, laughing gleefully.

Charlotte had risen in her excitement, and what she called her "gaudy hair" had dropped from its usual confinement, and her manner was almost fierce in her earnestness. The sight of Meg's gleeful clapping tickled her sense of humor.

"I declare, I'm ' orating' again, as Cuthbert calls it, and this darling even sees the absurdity." She caught up the child with a gay laugh, and when seated and her hair fastened again she said quietly, "Molly knows how warmly I feel on these points. I mean the necessity there is for a high standard of work and a determination to reach it. But seriously, if your daughter wishes to begin business on a small scale at once, I would advise her to make a little money as she goes along by raising radishes and salad to be ready just when they bring a high price. I know the people here would be glad to have

somewhere to send when there is nothing to be
got in these stores but carrots and turnips and
canned things; and the Woman's Exchange in
New York will take early radishes, lettuce, country butter, honey, provided they are all *better*
than the average, and I am sure they would take
cut flowers in time."

"I am almost inclined to go into the kitchen
garden business myself," said Mrs. Lennox,
laughing, as she rose and folded her work.
"Now I am going to tell Mary all I have heard.
I am inclined to think that she will listen with a
good deal more heart than to anything we have
yet mooted to her."

"Give my love to her, and tell her if her pansies beat Spink's " (Spink was the solitary Greenfield florist), "I'll be a good customer; if they
don't, I'll none of them. Oh, and tell her if
she starts her pond-lilies, I'll get her some bulbs
of the famous Boston pink lilies which no one
can buy."

"Thank you very much," said Mrs. Lennox.
"I am really almost sanguine myself that she
may succeed."

"Molly," said Charlotte, after Mrs. Lennox
had gone, "I've come to lunch, and I'm awfully
hungry. I always am when I come here, because I'm sure to find the unexpected."

"You will, this morning, in the shape of

scraps. There is cold veal, a little cold white-fish which I told Marta to warm up with the cold drawn butter and an egg beaten in it, and, of course, there's lettuce."

"Why, that's quite a swell lunch."

"Well, the fish is n't enough for two hungry people; there was n't more than two or three tablespoonfuls, but if you'll make some mayonnaise, we'll improve the veal into a salad."

Molly perceived Marta at the corner of the piazza making signs to her.

"Lunch is ready, I have no doubt, and Marta is wondering how we are going to manage, or whether I will dare to ask you to divide a spoonful of picked-up fish with me; she will never get used to 'pot luck.' We'll relieve her mind at once."

They went into the cool and pretty dining-room. Annie carried Meg away to be made neat, and Mrs. Welles, seeing the high chair, said, as she prepared to make the mayonnaise, "Have you promoted Meg to appear at table?"

"Yes, she sits very quietly, and if she has her little meal by me I see the way she eats. I don't want her to form slobbering habits, and she begins to handle a spoon quite well; of course, Annie or I are ready to help her in case of difficulty."

As she spoke, Molly was shaving the veal in

tiny little slices with the carving-knife, which
was always kept sharp as a razor, and as they
curled up over her knife she dropped them into
the center of the dish of lettuce; when there
was quite a little heap she seasoned it with salt
and pepper, and when Mrs. Welles had the
mayonnaise ready she spread it over the meat,
and the veal salad, almost equal to chicken, was
made.

When they were seated, and Meg had her little chop and baked potato, which Annie cut very
fine for her, Mrs. Welles said, "You ought to
get Meg one of those nice little trays that come
nowadays for children. I will get her one."

"Oh, please don't. Meg is to learn to eat so
cleanly that she will not need it. My mother
used to say such things as bibs and trays pro-
longed the time of untidy feeding, because one
is unconsciously less watchful if the bib only is
soiled or the tray, and the child soon knows it
must not soil frock or pinafore, while the bib is
only put on to be soiled. Annie, too, will be
more careful in not letting her drop food if it is
to fall on cloth or dress."

"But until she does learn?"

"Well, you will see she really makes very
little mess. If she has broth or soup, Annie
steadies the spoon; the same with oat-meal porridge or mush. Her clean pinafore is not put

on till after lunch, for the present, and if the table-cloth suffers, a napkin is put on just as if I or Harry made a spot. There is one under her plate now."

"Well, Molly, there may be something in what you say, but I'm afraid I should prefer bibs."

Meg did eat very neatly. There was a small collection of potato crumbs on the cloth round her and a little milk on her pinafore, which Molly pointed out to her, but with a little shocked look that, baby as she was, she understood; she also shook her head and deplored the mess.

Mrs. Welles had always laughed heartily at Molly's "training the baby," but she had looked with pleasure at the handling of the spoon. She had fully expected to see her turn it bowl upwards long before it reached her mouth, but generally it arrived at its goal with all its contents. When it was in danger of capsizing, Annie gave just enough aid to prevent it, and with spoon food this support was given to every mouthful.

"And do you go through that little performance of deploring the mess every day, Molly?" asked Charlotte, after Meg had gone to have her slip changed.

"Yes, almost. Meg and I mourn over it together, but the idea is well grounded in her little mind already that great care is to be taken, and when a big accident happens, or there is more mess than usual, we both make a great time over it."

"Yet it really seems to me that if you were to let Annie feed her for a year or so, you would have no mess at all."

"Oh, yes, I should; in fact, there would be rather more of it. You notice how many children who are fed will turn away their heads to look at something just as the spoon is close to their mouths. I know one little boy at four years old who has a devoted nurse; his attention is never fixed on what he eats, everything attracts him, and the spoon follows his movements, so that wherever his mouth happens to be, there is the spoon ready to pop into it.

"That, of course, is an extreme case. All I mean is, that if a child is allowed to handle a spoon herself, or with such slight aid as makes her believe she is doing so, her mental, or, perhaps, at such an age, one might say her 'instinctive,' act and her manual one help each other. Of course I may be all wrong. One can't argue from experience with one child. Meg may be unusually quick in using her hands, only I must tell you Mrs. Lennox says at two and a half years old her children fed themselves neatly without assistance."

" Did she use bibs ? "

" No, she had trays, but no feeding bib, and says she is quite sure the tray hindered habits of neatness; there was no special care to avoid slopping the tray.

" I expect, with Meg, to have a few accidents, to have a few extra napkins and cloths soiled, for a few months, and once in a while, I suppose, an extra slip, but you know they are not trimmed, so they add little to the work, and I am sure she will eat neatly much quicker if we are all on our guard, than if we give her bib and tray and take little notice of mishaps."

CHAPTER V.

MOLLY THINKS BACK.

MR. and Mrs. Bishop had been two years in their new home, and had enjoyed a very happy, bright, and prosperous time, to which every day seemed to bring new pleasure. Meg was developing very pretty ways, began to make odd little speeches, and was altogether a wonder and delight to her parents. But through all this joy Molly had been uneasily conscious of a crumpled rose leaf. She had said, when Mr. Bishop's means were unexpectedly increased, that they would not change their mode of living except so far as keeping a nurse made a change. She had then added nurse's wages and cost of board to her former estimate, and also the expense of gas, which in the new house would take the place of kerosene, and a considerable increase in the cost of fuel; for, although the house they now had was not large, it would take nearly twice as much fuel to heat it as the little cottage in which they had spent their first months of housekeeping, where there was but just room in the hall for a stove which tempered the air of the whole house and made the large fires in the rooms little necessary except on very cold days. But in the new house there was the furnace, which burned more coal itself than all the fires in the cottage, and seemed only just sufficient to keep the large hall and staircase and dining-room warm. In cold weather they still needed a parlor fire and two up-stairs, besides the kitchen.

However, these were the legitimate expenses of occupying a house built on a much larger scale; but Molly had awakened, at the end of the first year in the house, to the fact that their expenses had doubled. The first year Molly kept house she had kept rigid account; but the baby came, and for three months after it had not seemed so necessary, as they were going into the new house, and she knew exactly what she would spend; but after settling down with so inexperienced a nurse, it had been very easy to drift along from week to week and month to month without the accounts. Harry had been to blame, partly, for when she had expressed regret for her negligence and declared her intention of turning over a new leaf at once, he would say :

" My dear girl, I would n't. You know what you spend. Pay your butcher and grocer once a week ; keep an eye on their accounts. You get the gas, coal, and milk bills, and really, in such a small way of living as ours, the accounts almost keep themselves. We are not now limited to a dollar or two. While I had a stated salary and five dollars a month expended beyond a certain sum meant debt, and before many such ,months, disaster, it was all very necessary, but now the few dollars, more or less, will not ruin us."

Molly shook her head. She knew his reasoning, though kind, since he thought of her ease and pleasure, was not sound, but she allowed herself to drift. Meg was very enticing; she knew the child did not really prevent her doing anything that she had formerly done, but it is much easier to leave undone than to do.

For some little time before Meg was born, and, necessarily, some time after, she had given up going to market herself. The butcher called for orders, as he did on nearly all the neighbors. At first her orders had been carefully and exactly attended to, and though she felt she lost much by not being able to take advantage of the market as she could by seeing, she yet submitted to the inevitable. But somehow the habit of personal marketing had never been taken up again. She had not gone with Harry every morning to the depot after Meg was born; not because she couldn't do it, for Marta would always attend to the baby, even before Annie came, but because it did require some little resolution. Though Molly was anything but a self-indulgent or indolent woman, when duty was plain to her, she yet easily strayed away from the narrow path in which she forced herself to walk where need was evident, into broader and more flowery ways, and took no heed of her steps.

But now, at the end of two years, a little thing, only reading in a newspaper how much a mother had saved for her child by putting away five cents every day from the time she was born until she was twenty-one, aroused her. It did not touch her own experience at all, but it set her thinking, and when Harry had eaten his dinner that evening and had lighted his cigar she said with an unusually grave air, for Molly was something of a laughing philosopher and seldom very grave :

" Harry, are you too tired to talk seriously a little while ? " —

He looked at her in surprise.

" My dear Molly, of course not. Am I ever too tired, and don't I always talk seriously ? "

" You are not doing so now," Molly retorted. " However, I want to ask you one thing : do you think we live very much better than we did in the Winston cottage ? "

" No, I don't."

" Well, we spend a hundred dollars a month more than we did there."

" I know it, and have wondered, but I said nothing, for we are well within my income, and I think you have an easier time."

" I discover what I have before suspected, and that is, that I am naturally a very easy-going and indolent person. The last two years I have been negligent. I spent this afternoon in going over my bills to find the leak, but I cannot put my finger on any one thing, yet, in one month, I easily found fifteen dollars in mere trifles that we should have done without, and been quite as well without, when we were living within a certain limit."

" But, my dear, we only do as our neighbors do, and there is no need of living within the same severe limit. I don't believe there is waste."

" Well, the fact is, I am, perhaps, very greedy, but I must say I like to enjoy all I can afford. But we are not enjoying ourselves to the extent of a hundred dollars a month. When we came to this house I doubled our coal bill in my own mind, thought of Annie, in fact, added five hundred a year to our expenses, and if I had done in this house as I did in the other, that is to say, if every scrap of food had passed under my eye, it would have sufficed, and we should apparently have lived as well as now, because I have really been economical. I mean I have not ordered the things I would have liked many times, because of the expense. Now if we are to spend fifty dollars a month more than needful, let us do it knowingly and enjoyingly."

" Nonsense, Molly; really two thousand a year is very little to spend, living as we do, for we have two servants and every comfort."

"I don't care; if I return to my old ways, you 'll see either that we have a good many little luxuries we do without now, or we will have money saved. I don't mean to say that there has been extravagance, but the best has not been made of things. There is no sense, for instance, in paying twenty-eight cents a pound for veal, as I find by this week's bill it is, when, by waiting three weeks, the very same meat will be only eighteen cents. I forgot to ask the man the price of veal, and although in May it is usually the cheapest meat, it is, this year, very dear. Then I see, during the past year, I have bought chickens at twenty-five cents a pound. It is not a very terrible extravagance, and yet there is just the difference between good and bad management. I am willing, for a treat, to pay forty cents a pound for a broiler, but I want to feel while doing it that I really am having a luxury."

Harry laughed heartily.

" I confess I do not see the difference, Molly."

" I do. I have heard numbers of English and Americans wonder where the French of small means find the money for things that they, who are much richer, can't afford. A French family can oftener go to the opera, or dine at a first-rate restaurant, or hire a carriage, than people of much larger incomes. But it is just because they do their extravagance deliberately, and enjoy it to the full. Now I am going to turn over a new leaf, and once more see to everything myself ; above all, I shall go to market."

" Well, but can't you shut down on something ? If Marta slings things, tell her you will not have it. Don't make a slave of yourself."

" I don't mean to do that, I never did yet; and poor Marta does not ' sling things,' as you call it ; and there is absolutely no one special thing to ' shut down on,' only things are not made to go just as far as they will. It is difficult to say just where retrenchment may come in, but it is in every single thing, probably."

Molly was as good as her word, and the next morning she started to market. In after-years she wondered at herself. How could she possibly have managed without seeing the meat she wanted before it was cut? Why had she drifted into shirking (for that was the uncompromising word she used) a duty that she after all enjoyed when she set about it. It may as well be said here that Molly never again slipped back into an easy-going acquiescence. The shock of finding (once she roused herself to the task of examination) that money could so sift away and leave so little trace, that with an economy that refused self-indulgence on many little points, there yet should have been so much spent in avoidable trifles, had startled her so that never again did she backslide.

Mrs. Welles had remonstrated on her severity to herself, reminding her that two thousand dollars a year was a very moderate amount, and that they got quite as much out of it as most people.

"Yes, Charlotte, that is very true, but unfortunately, you see, I can, by using time which I have abundance of, make the money go half as far again, and not to do it is certainly to wrap my one small talent in a napkin."

In the days of her misfortunes how thankful she was to remember that, once having seen the line of her duty, she followed it; that she had not to reproach herself with continued negligence.

But the night that she decided to turn over a new leaf she made her resolutions at Meg's bedside. It was her custom to hear her prayers, and then to tell her some little story or verses before she left the room. This evening, however, after she had heard her prayers and tucked her up, she sat silent for a minute thinking, when Meg brought her to herself by saying, as she snugly settled herself :

"More cock-robin prayers, peas, mamma."

Molly looked at the rosy little one for a moment puzzled, then she laughed, for she understood that, to Meg, prayers and stories were all one.

CHAPTER VI.

MOLLY ENGAGES A NURSE — A DOUBTFUL TREASURE.

IT will be needless to tell the friends of Molly Bishop that no part of her furnishing interested her more than her kitchen. To have every needful thing, and not one useless one, was what she studied. I wish space would allow me to describe the cosy kitchen, but that I cannot do, yet I will say that as it was small, corner closets of pine were put up at convenient height to hold articles that would not be often used, and encumber the kitchen closet — such as fruit jars, etc.; these took no floor space. Over the kitchen table was a broad shelf, well out of the way of anything that might be standing on it, yet within easy reach, on which to set any finished articles and those that would be wanted too soon to warrant them being carried to the safe, etc. In her search for furniture, Molly had found an old-fashioned, gay-colored hearth rug, very cheap, because, although so out of date, it was of good make. This she had bought to

lay before the table when work was done, and
a bright red, ingrain table-cover gave a cosy,
homelike look to the room. She would have
liked a small rocker for Marta's comfort, but in a
sixteen by sixteen kitchen such a thing would be
a perpetual stumbling-block. She got, instead, a
folding chair, with carpet back and seat, that
was easier for sewing than the ordinary kitchen
chair.

When all the delightful fuss of purchasing
and settling down was over, Molly had to think
of the nurse that their means now justified her
in having. It had been a subject of much comment among her friends, and some ridicule on
the part of her mother-in-law, that she had not
engaged a nurse before the toil of moving into
the new house was undertaken.

Molly had learned that to be constantly ex-
plaining reasons and justifying her actions to
Mrs. Bishop senior, placed her in the position of
seeming to think herself wiser than others. She
generally thought out her course, but to explain
this process made her feel as if she must seem
very " preachy," so she simply left her to " wonder at Molly," and at Harry indulging such
freaks. How could that darling baby be properly tended, with Molly " up to her eyes in work."
But the baby flourished, nevertheless, and lay
on the mattresses or rugs, and rolled and kicked

and sometimes cried while Marta and Molly got the rooms in order. But although she would not explain reasons to her critics, she answered her affectionate friends' remonstrances frankly enough.

" To tell the truth, Charlotte, there is nothing terrible about it. If Harry had been in his old position I would never have thought of a nurse, and should have been obliged to do what I now do from choice; but I shall have a nurse for two reasons: I believe in doing everything that is *necessary* thoroughly and cheerfully, even if it is a task taking all one's strength, or if it be the greatest drudgery, but I do not believe in wasting one's self *unnecessarily* for the sake of saving twelve dollars a month and a little food. Another reason, I have a feeling that if you have the means of employing one unemployed woman it is a sort of duty to do it."

"Then why not have performed that duty already and saved yourself?"

" In the first place, I have enjoyed the work; the baby is absolutely well and of course is very good. But my chief reason is that I intend to take a perfectly green girl, the more inexperienced the better."

"Oh, Molly, what a notion! You have a partial success in Marta, — for I cannot see myself that a girl you have to follow and watch *is* a treasure, — but you may not find another Marta."

"You don't do justice to my poor Marta," laughed Molly; "the fact is, as servants go in this country, I am well satisfied. When the whole system is improved we may hope for some ability in addition to good intentions."

"Well, then, why would not even a green girl be better than nothing?"

"Because, if I had such a one, I could teach her nothing while so busy; besides, when people are unsettled, one has to make shift in many ways, and a week, if it be the first week, of unsettled living in the semi-picnic style inevitable, before things get into a settled way, would demoralize her so that it might take months to make her see what our ways really are, first impressions are so strong. But it is not only that; I want to have leisure to teach her all my ways and have nothing to unteach."

"There is a great deal in that; I admit that the process of unlearning seems to be the most difficult possible; one would think when that comes to be tried that their brains were as 'wax to receive and adamant to retain;' yet, when one tries to teach them, the case is very different, — the wax is lard and will receive no permanent impression."

Mrs. Bishop had found the one servant she

had at Castle Garden, and taught her everything she knew. Very much of her teaching had slipped from the girl, yet she retained enough to make her a fair cook. She ought to have been a very fine one. Yet Molly did not believe she would have done as well had she taken a young woman who had been long in the country and learned to do a few things badly. At any rate the result of her experiment was to encourage a repetition, and once the house was in perfect order Molly went to find a nurse.

Marta being German, she thought it would be better to go to Castle Garden the day on which she was most likely to find one of the same nationality. I confess she had in her mind's eye some fair-haired Gretchen, such as she had so often seen in Germany (so few of whom seem to arrive in this country in all the thousands that come), in whose arms it would be a pleasure to see her darling; but, as when she engaged her square, solid Marta, she had pictured a bright, intelligent girl, so now there were no Gretchens, — only toil-worn, hard-featured or stupid-looking women. In vain the matron pointed out one dazed creature after another. Not one did Molly think would suit. At last, just as she was about to give up for that morning, she saw in a corner a small figure with her head buried in the bundle beside her. Molly crossed to her and spoke.

She was very young, dark, and thin, and she looked stupidly up, yet the face was not stupid. Molly questioned her, found she was a German Swiss, that she had a terrible headache, and that her brother, with whom she had come, had gone off to a farm in Connecticut. She showed a letter from a pastor of the canton from which she came, testifying to her respectability and industry, and Molly engaged her, although, from certain indications, she doubted if she was quite clean. She had a grimy frill round her neck, and her skin and hands had an unwashed look.

"Yet, poor soul, landed only a few hours, with a headache and perhaps a heartache, one cannot expect much ; at all events I must risk it, and will not let her take the baby till I see."

Molly shuddered at the idea of her wholesome, dainty baby being in the arms of any one who was not very clean.

When she reached home she was amused to see the way Marta eyed the unpromising appearance of her new domestic, whose name was Anna. She could but remember her own misgivings when she engaged Marta.

But before a week passed she found that Anna had a fault Marta never had, — she was not clean ; and Molly was puzzled, for the girl was obedient, more than willing, anxious even, to work. Dirty habits had always, in Molly's experience hitherto, seemed, if not caused by, at least allied to, laziness.

"I hardly know what to do about Anna," she said to her neighbor and intimate friend, Mrs. Lennox. "She is quite well educated, far more intelligent than the average of her class, and yet I cannot let her take the baby."

"I don't think you will have any peace with a dirty girl."

"No, it seems rather hopeless; yet there are so many things I like about her, I am inclined to try what I can do with her. Surely, as she appears not to mind work, she would not mind bestowing a little of it on her own person."

Molly felt almost as much diffidence in approaching the subject as if Anna had been one of her own class. It seemed a very different thing to tell a girl that her dishes were not properly washed, or her sweeping was not thorough, or even to say she had to wear cleaner aprons, from what it was to tell her her hair was dirty though smooth, that her skin was unwashed, and all her belongings needed thorough cleansing. Many a housekeeper knew what all this was, and had had to correct even worse personal habits, but to Molly it was a new experience. So far as it was possible she wished to respect her servants, and to treat them as she herself would wish to be treated, and it was this fellow-feeling that made her picture the mortification of the girl. However, it was something she would have to hear if she was to live with any respectable family, and she nerved herself to the task.

Poor Molly almost wished Anna would do something to make her a little angry; what she had to say would come easier, — for Molly was a bit of a moral coward, as her husband would laughingly tell her. But beyond the chronic frowsiness of Anna's person and the fact that the first time she performed any task it was very ill done (the second much better), she could find no reasonable fault; so she had to begin her objurgation in cold blood.

She had given the baby its tepid bath, for this was a task she delighted in and always did herself, and the plump little thing was sweet and fresh and dainty as a white flower.

Anna had been instructed to put every single article back in its appointed place, to air the little night garments and fold them neatly, but the delicate flannel wrapper was already looking soiled from her handling.

"Anna," said Molly, gently, "I want to speak to you. Do you notice that, although I engaged you to nurse the baby, I never give her to you?"

Anna flushed. "I do notice, ma'am, and I thought perhaps I did not please you."

The words were spoken timidly, and the girl's face showed her distress.

" The fact is, Anna, you are not clean enough.
If you were to carry the baby I should have to
change her clothes twice a day."

" Not clean! " cried the girl in amazement,
and then she pressed both hands on her hair,
which was tightly braided, and looked down at
her woolen dress, which was without a rent, and
patched neatly enough, where worn.

"I don't believe the poor thing knows what
it is to be clean," thought Molly.

" I know you are tidy enough, but don't you
know that you have to wash your clothes and
your skin ? I noticed yesterday you took up the
ashes in this room and then, *without washing*
your hands, began to strip the baby's cradle,
until I reminded you. You must wash your
hands after every dirty task that soils them.
The white aprons I have given you are soiled
almost immediately, not by the work you do, but
by your hands and dress. I am not scolding
you, but if you leave me you will find the same
trouble elsewhere."

Even as Molly talked she felt a sort of despair
of reforming a girl with whom she had to begin
by telling her when to wash her hands, and
realized after all if even her gown and hands
were clean, how little that was when her hair
seemed glued with oil and dirt.

" I always have been thought clean, but I will
do anything you tell me, ma'am."

Tears were in the girl's eyes, and Molly believed she meant what she said.

"Very well, Anna; I will help you to change your habits if you will obey. You must have that gown washed and put on your best. I will buy some seersucker for two dresses, and cut and fit them for you. Can you use a sewing-machine?"

"A little."

"Very well; I will show you what you do not know. Your first wages must be spent to get you the proper changes."

For the next month Molly had to devote much time to Anna. She found the girl quite willing, but unable to realize that once clean she must keep so. A bath taken was something to be repeated only at very long intervals, and she told Molly her hair had never been washed since she was a child because she would take cold. Nevertheless, by degrees she became used to washing her hands, and to the fact that her dress must not be worn till it was black before it was washed.

Marta was the worst disappointment to Molly at this time. She had looked to her to be good to the stranger, and to help her over the first difficulties, but it was easy to see that Marta despised her utterly. Her dirtiness was perhaps the beginning of this, and the prejudice once entertained was not to be got rid of; and long after Molly had ceased to distrust her and she had taken up her duties, Marta found fault, and by reason of her older standing in the family, queened it over her. Yet Molly's own belief was that if she had spent as much time teaching Anna as Marta, the intelligence of the former would have given better results.

Another reason, perhaps, for Marta's contempt for Anna was the discovery soon made that the latter took refuge in a lie as naturally as a duck takes to water. She seemed to expect to be scolded for every trivial fault, and denied it instantly, as a child sure of being whipped might. Sometimes, not to humiliate her, Molly pretended to be unaware of the lie. At others she talked seriously and kindly to her, pointing out that her untruths deceived no one, recalling one or two instances in which she had disbelieved her without saying so, but that they doubled the fault; reminding her, too, that she would not be scolded for accidents or mistakes; that even if she had some serious mishaps she would only aggravate the evil by a falsehood.

"Indeed, Anna, I should be more inclined to send you away for the untruth than the misfortune."

The girl wept bitterly, and assured Mrs. Bishop she should never regret having patience

with her, that no one had ever been so kind.
To Molly, who watched her so closely, it was a
very sad proof of the result of severe treatment
on a timid nature. The result is almost always
deceit. From questions she learned that her
mother had been a good, industrious woman who
worked in a lace factory, and for years Anna had
also done the same work, but that she had pun-
ished every small fault. The girl artlessly told
this as a proof of her mother's excellence, not as
a cruelty to herself.

There is no gainsaying the fact that Anna was
a very unpromising servant, yet she did improve,
and Molly had helped herself to be patient by
remembering how often a fairly competent servant will deteriorate, and so she resolved to give
this poor, good, willing soul a fair trial.

One reason stronger than all others with
Molly for taking an entirely inexperienced girl
for nurse was because she had her own theories
about the bringing up of her child, and a nurse
who pretended to have experience would be
likely to act on that experience covertly, if she
did not do so openly. Molly had a strong conviction, gathered from what she had observed
and what she had read, that on the first year of
a child's life depends very much more of its
character as a child than on the second year.

Usually mothers think it is early enough to
begin training a child when it has passed its first

year, often its second. The cunning little ways
that, coming from a midget just able to crawl,
are so irresistibly funny, become very naughty
tricks when the child is two years old, and one
day the poor baby is frowned upon and scolded
for actions that have heretofore been laughed at
and often followed by rapturous kisses of delight
from mamma. But baby's habits have been
formed, young as it is, and it has to unlearn,
which is a very hard process for grown people,
who see the reason for it, but harder for a little,
unreasoning being, who only understands that it
is being smiled at and loved, or frowned upon
and chilled, without knowing why.

Molly dreaded spoiling her baby. Every
one, at first, had predicted that it would be
trained to death. There had been a rapid som-
ersault of opinion. At first it had been thought
that with her ideas of training a baby from the
first (those ideas, reader, were newer when
Molly's baby was born than they are to-day) she
would be a cold, hard mother; then when they
saw how she reveled in her little one, how constantly she tended it herself, there was a certainty that it would be spoiled, especially when
they neither heard nor saw that the derided
"training" was carried beyond the first month.

Nevertheless, Molly did keep a watch over
herself and the little Margaret; she was careful
to discourage her doing anything at six months

that she would have to check at two years, and
so when the baby eyes were caught by glittering
ornaments, and the baby hands outstretched for
them, the little hands were gently put down.
Anna and Marta and even Mr. Bishop thought
there could be no harm in indulging baby with
unbreakable objects from the mantel, but Molly
shook her head.   And so it was with tearing
books.   Anna discovered baby liked nothing so
well as to tear paper, and gave it a sheet of
newspaper to play with.   Molly saw the baby
tearing and scattering and delighting in the
noise it made, and gently coaxed the sheet away.

"Oh, but she loves to have it," said Anna
when she saw the action.

"Yes; but what difference can baby see between the paper it may tear and that which it
may not? and later she will naturally tear every
book she can get hold of, and then, poor darling, we should have to scold, and she would cry
to do what she has always been allowed to do, —
would n't you, my precious?"   And then Molly
poured out a flood of mother eloquence over the
darling, and, as every mother has her own love
language, it is of no use to describe Molly's,
which was in no sense wiser than any one else's.

But this was the gist of Molly's training:
that prevention was better than cure; that if
the child was not allowed to acquire bad habits,
there would be none to cure.

CHAPTER VII.

I⊤ is not my intention to dwell very long on this sunny part of Molly's life. The clouds that were to darken it later had not yet cast their shadows upon her, and the smooth by-way of perfect happiness is a very uninteresting road to those wayfarers who like the bustle and traffic and excitement of the busy highway of life.

I will say shortly, therefore, that although Molly was careful to tell herself that from this one child she could not judge others or even another, yet so far as this one was concerned she had reason to congratulate herself. By the time it was a year old it was generally conceded that it was a wonderful baby.

About this time Molly and her husband made a trip to Chicago, and when she emerged the first morning from the sleeper, with the baby dressed and bathed and happy, she was looked upon with curiosity; and one old gentleman who occupied the section next to hers, said :

" I congratulate you, madam ; that is the only

really good baby I ever traveled with. Last night when I saw you were my neighbor I made up my mind to the usual thing, but I never heard the child."

Molly was far happier than if he had said her baby was the most beautiful he had ever seen, but although she was a very proud young mother at that moment, she concealed her elation and said half apologetically, for there were other babies on board who were by no means quiet:

" But my baby has nothing to cry for, she is so perfectly well."

When Harry came to take her to breakfast, she gleefully told him what the old gentleman had said.

Mr. Bishop, however, seemed to take it as a matter of course.

" Well, Molly, you knew she was a good baby, did n't you?"

" Oh, yes, I thought so; but you know every mother thinks her own baby good, and friends agree with her; but this gentleman actually goes out of his way to tell me so, and it *is* pleasant, I confess."

An hour or two later a young lady whose baby had fretted very much during the night, and was now only kept quiet by constant change of movement on the nurse's part, came and seated herself next to Molly. She looked tired and anxious.

"Will you excuse me if I ask you what you give your baby to soothe it?"

Molly hardly understood the purport of the question at first. When she did, she looked at the weary young mother in horror, which soon changed to pity.

"I give her nothing; why should I?"

"She was so quiet, I thought you might, and yet she seems so well and bright that if you did, I felt almost inclined to try. My poor baby is so restless and cries so incessantly that I and Mandy are quite worn out, and my husband is almost as bad, for he can't sleep."

"But there must be some cause. Have you consulted a physician?"

"Oh, yes; but he says the baby is well, and I suppose it is; and some say it is good for a baby to cry, but I can't think it; then it annoys other people so terribly. That lady," indicating a fine-looking elderly woman, "tells me it is cruel not to help the dear little thing to sleep, and it does seem so, yet I have heard such dreadful things of soothing syrups and cordials."

"Oh, I would not dose a child for the world. Drugs must injure the brain!"

"Oh, you can't tell what you would do if you had a baby that had cried night and day for ten weeks with hardly any intermission, especially if you were not very strong yourself." The young mother moved wearily away, and Molly did wonder what she would do if she were so tried. A little later, seeing the baby on its mother's lap, she went toward her and offered to relieve her.

The baby was in one of its rare quiet moods, and was certainly not an unhealthy-looking child. It was rather thin, but its skin was mottled. It was daintily clothed and evidently well cared for, and yet Molly felt certain that something was wrong about the care. She asked the mother if she thought its food was sufficiently nourishing, and was told that the doctor had said so; she gave it food made of condensed milk and prepared barley, which seemed to agree with it perfectly. At this point the elderly lady came near them.

"I have been advising this lady to give her baby a little soothing syrup. The child needs rest, and till it gets it, it will not get on." She looked inquiringly at Molly, who would rather have said nothing, and did not answer until directly asked the question; then she said:

"I can hardly say what I should do, but one thing I know I never would do, and that is give any kind of drug or cordial to a baby."

The lady drew her shawl a little closer about her and smiled indulgently.

" My dear, you have your first child, which happens to be a good one. I am the mother of seven, all robust, strong men. That is my youngest over there," pointing to a very tall, ruddy, broad-shouldered youth, " and I assure you," she said, smiling satirically, " I never allowed him to have a restless night when a teaspoonful of soothing syrup would give him a good one. I have six more such sons, and I firmly believe that soothing syrup saved the lives of two of them in teething ; there is n't a mother in our part of the country can show such a family as mine."

She looked triumphantly at Molly, who was of course dumb. What could she say — she with only her one wee lamb and her convictions — against the testimony of this experienced matron who could point to such a robust specimen of human nature as the result of dosing ? What she did say in her heart was, " They must indeed have been strong to have survived."

In spite of herself she could not help thinking of the poor crying baby and wondering what was wrong. She knew that there were nervous, restless babies that no care could change, but this particular one did not impress her so. The mother, too, in spite of her weariness, seemed of a placid temperament.

It chanced that when they reached the hotel

at which Mr. Bishop intended to stay the young mother and her baby were in the parlor. Later she found their rooms were close together; and all through the night they could hear the wail of the baby, and Molly's heart ached for both mother and child.

They met on stairs and corridor often for the next day or two, and always stopped to talk of the two babies; and on the third morning as Molly came from her breakfast she found Mrs. Stevens, the young mother, walking up and down the hall with her infant while the nurse was breakfasting.

"Won't you come into my room? I am just going to bathe Meg while Anna goes down."

"Oh, I would love to do it," said Mrs. Stevens. "I wish I had courage to wash Freddy; I am so afraid I might hurt him."

"Anna is not experienced or careful enough for me to trust her to bathe Meg, and I prefer to do it, for then I have no uneasiness."

"Mandy happily is very experienced, so I have no fear; and then she is devoted to the baby."

This Molly had observed for herself, and yet she felt Mandy was scarcely the person to be left to bathe an infant.

"Why don't you take courage and bathe him yourself, since you wish to do it. It is really only the first time you need dread."

Mrs. Stevens hesitated. " I wish I could, but Mandy would be hurt, and might be a little sulky, and I am sure I should be so scared the first time that I could not do it without assistance."

" Suppose you do it right now," said Molly, smiling. " Meg is very comfortable, and you use her water."

Meg was on the floor, rolling in perfect content, with a bunch of keys which always seemed more fascinating than the orthodox rattle. " If Mandy had to leave you for a day, or were ill, you would be glad to have taken the first step — or I will bathe it to-day, and you come here to-morrow."

Mrs. Stevens accepted the offer, and the baby was undressed, Molly admiring the exquisite quality of the little garments as they were removed, and their dainty make.

As it lay undressed, she saw the child was well formed and seemingly very healthy. It had cried of course during the whole process of undressing, and now as Molly, with rolled-up sleeve, was about to lay the tiny little form with her hand under its body, the head supported by her arm, in the water, the child raised its arms, and Molly uttered an exclamation : the arm-pits were entirely raw !

" Oh, the poor darling! No wonder it cried."

Further investigation showed that wherever two fleshy parts came together they were denuded of skin, and the flesh was angry and shining. Molly could hardly believe that since the baby had been in Mandy's care, water had ever been used to the crevices of the child's body.

The poor, shocked mother wept bitter tears to think how her darling must have suffered.

"Oh, how cruel Mandy was," she said, kissing the poor little limbs.

"I don't think she has intended to neglect it; probably she has barely noticed in washing the chafed spots, or has thought a little powder would set it right, but " —

Molly carefully washed the spots with warm water into which she had put a pinch of borax, dabbing the excoriated flesh with the child's own face-sponge, and drying it with soft old linen. She had meanwhile told the mother to take a half teaspoonful of powdered borax and rub it with the bowl of a teaspoon on paper till it was as fine and smooth as possible, then to mix it with three teaspoonfuls of talcum, and powder the child with it.

The child screamed through the whole process, but when it was over and Mrs. Stevens took it from Molly, without waiting for food, it fell asleep.

"Oh, what can I say to you and for myself ?

But I had examined its neck and did not find any sign of chafing, and thought if it was neglected I should see it there. You must think me a heartless mother, and yet I dearly love my baby."

"Of course you do, and I might have been no wiser with my own had I not heard a story of a nurse's neglect when I was a child, and knew ever after that the chafing of the skin was one of the very chief things to guard against."

"What would you advise me to do now?"

"I shall be here three or four days longer, and if you wish I will bathe the baby to-night and to-morrow; then I will be by you the first two times you do it yourself. I would certainly bathe it twice a day during this warm weather."

"I will do anything! How long do you think it will take to heal?"

"Oh, a very short time, I am sure, with such attention as you will give it; but I think in case the talc does not agree with its skin that I would get some Lycopodium, and use that in its place."

When Mrs. Bishop left Chicago she left one grateful friend there and one bitter enemy. Mandy angrily resented the "meddlesomeness" which had betrayed her own unfitness for her place. But Molly's adventures with tiny Meg were not at an end. On the return journey the happy baby excited much comment and some sneers. It was rather singular, but Molly found a quiet baby was as much sneered at as a blue stocking used to be. One incident that tickled Harry's sense of fun hugely was the remark of a grave old lady, who said:

" Does n't that child ever cry ? "

"Oh yes, indeed she does. If she's uncomfortable she lets us know it; but then we try to keep her very comfortable, so her crying is not very frequent."

" Well, I dare say you're very proud of having a good baby, but mark my words that child will have no lungs! If I had a baby who did n't cry its full share I should make it. What sort of a chest will it have ? "

In speaking of this journey of Molly's I have somewhat anticipated. In her inexperience she had dreaded the weaning of little Meg, and again Mrs. Lennox had come to her aid.

" My dear, just before my first baby was born I read in " Scribner's Magazine " an article on weaning babies, which helped me to form a plan of my own. I will look it up, and you will perhaps be able to adapt the rules to your needs. I am certain of one thing, and that is, that the idea of gradually preparing the child to be weaned is a good one. As to the literal carrying out of the details, every mother must be guided by her own sense and circumstances."

This conversation took place when Meg was six months old, and already for several weeks Molly had given her a teaspoonful of the bowl of oatmeal gruel which she herself took at eleven each morning (for the baby's benefit), watching very keenly the first day or two the effect the food had on its bowels; but this was in every way good with Meg, who needed laxative food, although with many children the oatmeal might have been unsafe. Molly's object, however, was to familiarize the child with the use of a spoon, so that when feeding became necessary, a bottle need not be used.

She read the article that Mrs. Lennox had given her, and such parts of it as applied strictly to weaning she marked for her own guidance. They were as follows : —

"Many mothers put off the necessity of weaning the baby, yet are sadly conscious that they neglect a duty to themselves and the child by putting off the evil hour, — the mother-heart shrinking from what she feels must be pain to her darling. With tender prescience she sees the week of weeping and baby agony she will have to encounter. And so time goes on, and the child, who should have been weaned at between nine and twelve months, is unweaned at fifteen; indeed, among working women I have known them to be unweaned at two years!

"Of course there are babies and babies — it may not be possible to prescribe a rule for all cases ; the best age for weaning baby may come just as it is suffering from some infant trouble, in very hot weather, on the eve of a journey, — a dozen things, in short, may make it advisable to defer the time ; but for healthy children there is no age at which weaning is so easy to mother and child as from nine to twelve months of age, and the later it is after such age the more difficult.

"Yet need it be such a painful time ? I think not. I know that in the case of a healthy baby accustomed to being nursed at regular hours, there actually need be no trial to the child, provided the mother has patience and firmness — not even a tear. Foolishly fond mothers, who have used nature's food as a solace for every woe, will not perhaps find a tearless weaning possible ; but I write for those tenderly wise ones who have observed as regular hours for baby's meals as for their own ; or for those about to become mothers. To these last I would say: As you value your baby's health and comfort, your husband's ease, and your own nerves, *begin with the first day* and accustom the baby to nurse only at certain hours.

" A newly born baby will require food oftener than when older ; but constitutions differ so much that it is best to consult your doctor as to the number of meals it will require during the day, and then adhere *strictly* to his rules. This point is so often neglected, or the necessity for some rule for feeding being acknowledged, it is so often considered time enough to begin 'when baby gets older,' when it is a difficult matter to break habits formed, that for the sake of mother and child it cannot be too strongly urged. Physicians say, half the colicky babies are made so during the first month of their life, by the old school of monthly nurses or foolish mothers overfeeding them, or keeping them so warm that every breath of fresh air afterwards chills them.

" As the child gets older, gradually diminish the number of meals, letting it, however, take as much food as it cares for at each one, until at six months it has but four meals during the day from its mother and one at night. At that age it is well to begin feeding with a little oatmeal porridge or prepared barley food ; begin with a teaspoonful, gradually increasing the quantity till at nine months or thereabouts it will take a hearty meal of it. Of course every mother must be guided by the constitution of her child in the choice of food ; for one child will starve on what another will thrive on ; but avoid feeding entirely, or even principally, on cornstarch. The best hour for giving this extra food will also de-

pend on circumstances. A good plan is to nurse
the baby at eight A. M. and at noon, at four and
at seven P. M.; and at 10 A. M. give the oatmeal
or barley gruel. The first step in weaning will be
to break off one meal. The four-o'clock meal is
the best to wean from first; when the baby comes
in from its airing a cup of warm food may be
ready for it. It is well, if convenient, for the
mother to disappear the first time the substitu-
tion is made. Wait a week before weaning from
a second meal; then break off the noon nursing
in the same way, having the food quite ready
when baby comes in hungry. In mild weather,
the young child should be out every sunny hour
of the day; modern carriages enable it to sleep
as restfully as in bed. Let it get quite used to
this change before proceeding to another. The
weaning from the evening meal it is best to
leave till last. When it becomes time for this,
give simply as much warm new milk as the child
cares to take, then put it to bed as usual. There
is now but the night nursing left. This may be
broken off by giving a cup of warm milk the
moment it wakes, for a few nights, gradually de-
creasing the quantity till it will no longer wake
for it, but sleep till morning, when it is well to
give it as much milk as it wants. This may
seem a slow and tedious plan in the telling, but
it is not so in practice; to a tender-hearted

mother it is at all events preferable to the week of tears and struggles that follows weaning by the short and sharp method.

" One word more about feeding the baby. By giving its meals at certain hours and those only, one meal has time to digest before another is taken. You thus avoid a fruitful cause of colic. A baby, too, who is fed regularly only craves food at certain times, and then it will take a hearty satisfying meal, while one nursed every half hour is ever craving and restless; its stomach cannot digest the food so constantly introduced, and crying, wakefulness, and general misery are the result."

CHAPTER VIII.

LITTLE JOHN ARRIVES. — CLOUDS ON MOLLY'S HORIZON. — MOLLY A WIDOW.

MEG was nearly three years old when Molly's second baby was born, a boy this time, much to Mr. Bishop's delight, and at first to Meg's disgust. She felt that her nose was put sadly out of joint by the new-comer, and when she saw the baby lying by *her* mother, she quickly turned her back and could not be made to look at it again.

"Why, Meg!" said Mrs. Welles, "won't you look at your little brother?"

But Meg persistently turned the back of her curly head to the bed.

"What shall we do with little brother, then, Meg?"

"Put him in the coal-scuttle!" came decisively from the baby lips.

Molly was distressed at her darling's jealousy, but it did not last long. She ran to hide her face in her aunt Charlotte's lap (she called Mrs. Welles aunt), but gradually began to take surreptitious peeps when no longer invited to do so, and very soon she had toddled to the bedside. Molly showed the tiny pink hand and nails, and then Meg suddenly ran away. She soon reappeared, dragging all her own best raiment after her, and a pair of scarlet gloves, that were her delight, in her hand.

She struggled to the bedside, clutching the dainty white silk coat trimmed with fur, that had been her grandmother's Christmas gift, close to her, and the Normandy bonnet was trailing on the floor behind her.

"Bless her heart!" cried Mrs. Welles, starting to the rescue. "She is bringing her choicest for her brother."

And so she was; for fine as the coat and bonnet were, the gloves were the last purchase, and dearer to her than anything; the other things were forgotten as soon as she was relieved of them, but she darted to the bed with the gloves, and put one on the little screwed-up ball of a fist, saying as she did so, very gravely, "He shall have my cárlat gubs." After this there was no trouble; Meg seemed to think the baby was a larger sort of doll prepared for her amusement, and when Molly came down-stairs it was difficult to convince her that she could not have it to carry round and play with.

Little John, as they named the new baby, was

a baby without a history. Happy the nations, women, and babies who are so! It was almost exasperating too, for it disappointed many who had looked to this second baby to refute some of Molly's ways. Mrs. Bishop senior fell back on her son's constitution and temperament again to account for babies that persistently throve in the absence of sufficient food, or any proper medicine, or, in fact, bringing up of any kind. Molly herself had expected a totally different experience with this baby, knowing well how children differ; but except as months went on she found the difference in temperament between boy and girl was very strongly marked, there was not much for her to change in the bringing up of the two. Exactly as Meg had been about food, so was this child. He slept much less, but he was happy and good when awake, and nothing delighted him more than his bath, to which Meg had never taken kindly, until old enough to stand up in it and make fun for herself.

Molly thought she had so many blessings, that at times she had a fear there would be some drawback. And when this second baby came, so healthy, and good, and she herself so well, she wondered if she was to be exempt from all the trials that beset so many women — and what she had done to deserve a happiness that seemed so serene. We who know her recognize that she might easily have created a few miseries for herself, had her nature been less wholesome. But of late she was troubled with a vague uneasiness. Her husband had changed very much. He who was once so gay and pleasure-loving, now had been gradually becoming more and more absorbed in business. Molly was a brave wife and told herself that she could not expect her husband to differ from the generality of men who settled down into business harness. She had hitherto in her mind's eye seen herself and Harry going down life's hill, happy and merry as they were now. She had determined for her own part to make no artificial troubles; so she resolved to say nothing of his changed manner, to cheer him when she could, and when he preferred to bury himself in his newspaper, to leave her own wish to talk, or do anything else, unuttered.

But as months went on her own gay manner changed insensibly, for Harry grew every day more preoccupied and was almost morose at times. His happy laugh or hearty kiss for Meg at the gate was no longer the first intimation she had of his evening home coming. He passed both Meg and little John, whom once he had always brought into the house on his shoulders, with an absent-minded caress, and as they clung to his legs or fingers, he scarcely seemed to

know they were there as he quietly entered the
house and mechanically kissed Molly. Sometimes he would speak impatiently, almost crossly,
but then immediately he would gather the one
so spoken to, Molly or Meg, in his arms, and say
some tender, remorseful word that would show
poor Molly that his love was the same. Anxiously she would search his face sometimes, and
once or twice she had asked him if he was worried or had any trouble.

"My dear, business men always are worried
at times. I am no worse off than any other; but
you must not trouble your little head with my
glumness. Every man who goes on the cars
with me is as glum as an oyster; that is, if he
is not one of the irresponsible men of business
who live by making other business men believe
they are swimming in very smooth water."

"But you are so unlike yourself, Harry, I
can't help worrying about you."

"Then you must not Molly. These are very
serious times, and my father's health is so im-
paired that I have almost more than I can attend to. Don't look so anxious, dear; come,
let's say 'begone dull care' and send it to the
dogs. I do need something to shake me up;
come to New York this afternoon, Booth is
playing Hamlet."

Very gladly Molly agreed to go, hoping Harry

might throw off his moodiness, and for that night they enjoyed themselves. It did seem like old times when Harry made jokes in the cars as they came home, — and for a day or two Molly flattered herself that he was regaining his old light-heartedness; but then she found reason to fear that it was assumed for her benefit. She had long suspected he did not sleep so soundly at night as he pretended, that while she slumbered he lay awake; and when this suspicion became pronounced, her own sleep was very light, and she found he did lie awake for hours, and when he slept it was an uneasy, dreamy sleep with broken utterances that were all figures and business terms.

She felt sure now that he had troubles he kept from her. She spoke to him about their expenditure.

"Harry, let me know if we are spending too much money. You know we can always go back to our old limit, or half of it. Nurse is no absolute necessity, and in these hard times " —

Harry burst into laughter, yet not the old hearty, happy laughter; there was a sort of grim bitterness in it which wrung Molly's heart.

"My dear, do you know that my father spends $20,000 a year? my mother would not dream of living on less. Now, I have only a fifth share in our business; we spend less than half my income, but you can see for yourself that in so large a business, even if we saved a thousand dollars more a year, it would make no material difference. No, dear Molly, the few poor little hundreds that make the difference between hard work and ease for you would only be a drop in the ocean. Don't worry, dear, — we are doing right; if there is any worry, leave it to me."

" But, Harry, if there is worry let me share it."

He kissed her very tenderly, and told her, business men had always worries. "When there is any use in worrying you, dear, you shall have your share; but if a man in business were to tell his wife all that he has to think of, she would be frightened at possible issues, and he would be unnerved."

Molly could not agree with him, but neither would she argue; she knew she could not make her husband see with her eyes, and she allowed him to think that he had reassured her; but so far from doing so, she now felt certain that he kept some trouble from her. It seemed the wildest nonsense, only to be conjured up in a fanciful woman's brain, to fear that the old firm of Bishop, Whitehead & Bishop could be in difficulties. No, that she did not fear. Harry's father was a business man of the old school, cautious and conservative. Mr. Whitehead interfered very little, and the business had flourished for fifty years.

One thing might have accounted for Harry's changed manner, and that was his father's failing health, only that for two years past Mr. Bishop's share of the office work had devolved on his son, and had seemed to cause very little anxiety. There had later come a fear of softening of the brain, and the physicians had ordered him to travel, so as to be entirely away from business.

The old gentleman had decided to go to the wheat states, and to California. He had been absent six months, and the last few weeks he had been in Chicago. Mrs. Bishop sent her son encouraging accounts of his health, and these letters he passed over to Molly.

She thought and thought, haunted by a presentiment of evil, but not knowing where to look for the blow to come from. In this trouble she could have no confidant, or comfort ; not even to Mrs. Welles could she tell her anxieties. The latter saw the change in her blithe friend and wondered at it. But at this time she was not quite so observant as usual, for after six years of married life she was preparing baby clothes.

In one sense this was not only a joy to herself but a blessing to Molly, who entered with something of her old enthusiasm into her friend's hopes. Little John could now walk, and he and Meg would trot with Molly on the warm, bright

days to Mrs. Welles's piazza. Annie, who was
an excellent seamstress, was thus free to make
up the little garments which Molly cut and
fitted for her.

Molly's children, by the way, were noticeably
well dressed, with less trouble, perhaps, to mother,
nurse, or laundress than most children in the
same position.

Molly eschewed ruffles, and put the extra
goods that they would take into the quality, so
she had fine cambric frocks at about the same
cost as coarse. The clothes were all simply
made but most beautifully fitted; and Molly was
an eager watcher for picturesque patterns, such
as were pretty without regard to the fashion,
which a great authority says is the true test of
beauty in clothes; then they were very neatly
sewed and finished; where there was embroidery
or lace, it was small in quantity and fine in quality.

Mrs. Welles frankly told Molly that her baby
was to be a good old-fashioned one. It should
not be dosed, but she intended to rock it to sleep
and let it feed when it liked. "That's the way
I was brought up, and although your darlings
are models, I still think, my dear, they have
your own sweet, contented nature, and would have
been so anyhow; they are of the placid kind."

"Do you call John placid?"

"No, but he is a boy; he is good, but there

seems a good deal of the natural Adam in him, I confess."

Molly smiled; perhaps she alone knew how much of that natural Adam there was latent in her boy, how closely she was watching him, and checking the first little tendency to fault, before it became a fault. A raised finger, a grave look now, would save graver punishment later. But all this little motherly strategy could not be explained, it could only be observed by one interested in noticing closely. She remembered one indignant young mother who had said:

"That just maddens me, — people say, 'Oh, but *your* child has such a lovely disposition, you can't judge of other children by that one!' As if its disposition wasn't human, and as if I had n't been watching like a lynx to repress its little bad ways and encourage its good ones; and then when he does n't cry for the moon, and is a happy cherub as babies were meant to be, I am told it's all owing to his own placid nature!"

Molly was by no means angry about it, as was her young friend, but she was quietly amused.

"I foresee, Charlotte, you are going to introduce a small Moloch and sacrifice yourself on its altar."

"I am willing; but, my dear Molly, if my baby

should be a tyrant it will only show the natural depravity of some infants."

The conversation was carried on laughingly. Mrs. Welles's good-humor was rarely ruffled, and Molly really believed her warm-hearted friend would enjoy lavishing herself upon an outrageous baby. And so the event proved.

Never was a child endowed with such lungs, and such power of gaining its will with them, as little Lois Welles. Before it was three months old it had learned to cry for everything it craved, but as there seemed only two things that what Harry called the little " Mollusk " can crave at that age, its mother's arms and its mother's food, and its mother delighted in satisfying it, there was no difficulty. Mrs. Welles showed her fine white teeth with her heartiest laugh when the impatient baby resented even a moment's delay in satisfying it, by making itself rigid from head to heel, and lifting its body into a small arc, and knocking its own poor little nose with its fists in its rage.

" Did you ever see such a spirited little thing. I know you 're shocked, Molly, but I love its antics, and so does Cuthbert. (Cuthbert was Mr. Welles's name.) It is so deliciously absurd to see such a helpless mite in a rage ! "

Molly was n't a bit shocked.

Mrs. Welles was a woman of large means,

perfect in health, and of the sweet, easy-going temperament that half-a-dozen spoilt children would not have *worried*, although they might have *wearied* her. Mr. Welles might, if there should be a second child that exacted all its mother's time, feel some right to it himself, but at present he was absorbed in watching the* growth and development of this one, and if the development was in the direction of temper it was but the more amusing.

As I have said, considering Mrs. Welles's health, temperament, and financial position, Molly was not shocked nor worried for her. She did not by any means think that spoilt babies or spoilt children made bad men and women, provided the spoiling did not extend to weak indulgence toward any moral laxity. Although still a young woman, Molly had lived long enough to see children whose parents and friends had been martyrs, of whose future terrible predictions had been made, grow out of their faults and make particularly nice boys and girls, and she had no fear for Mrs. Welles's children. She knew her friend would indulge them in everything that called only on her own or her servants' patience, but when it came to the formation of their character she would carefully watch them, and be firm enough in checking any evil tendency. She herself did not care to be a mar-

tyr for the first years of her children's life.
And had Mrs. Welles been a woman with many
of life's burdens, it would have troubled Molly
to see her deliberately creating fresh ones, which
would wear her life away; but Charlotte Welles
being what she was, situated as she was, she was
amused to see her gleeful motherhood.

Her own children were a great solace to poor
Molly in these days, for as months went by
Harry's mood did not change; or, rather, he did
have spells of more than his old gayety, but they
did not deceive his loving wife. She guessed
too truly that it was put on for her benefit.

She was so preoccupied that she did not ob-
serve Charlotte's anxious look at her one day
that she tore herself away from the absorbing
Lois. Mrs. Welles's visit was consequent on a
conversation which had passed between herself
and husband the evening before.

"I'm afraid Bishop, Whitehead & Bishop
are in serious trouble," said Cuthbert, "and that
accounts for Harry's changed ways. I have
feared it some time."

"What do you mean? You can't mean they
are about to fail? I thought it was considered
one of the most stable firms in this country!"
cried Charlotte.

"So it is, or was; but a madman can swamp
the stoutest ship if he bores a hole in it, — and

old Bishop's brain was giving way a year ago.
He ought never to have been in a position since
to sign the firm name, but I expect, though he
got physically better on his travels, he has men-
tally broken down. His pompous fool of a
wife has n't enough brain herself to see it, so he
has been practically unchecked."

"But tell me quickly what has happened.
Think of dear Molly."

"Nothing has happened, and I trust nothing
may. Young Bishop is a power and may succeed in keeping the firm afloat, but the fact is,
for some time past it has been known that the
old man has been speculating in wheat. This
surprised every one who knew the traditions of
the firm, and there came heavy losses; nothing,
however, very serious until to-day, when there is
a report that old Mr. Bishop has bought enor-
mously of wheat, for a rise. Those Chicago
fellows have got hold of him, and as he has re-
cently been over the wheat-growing districts, I
suppose he thought himself a match for them;
at all events, there is a tremendous fall in wheat,
and it is said that a million will not cover the
Bishops' loss."

Charlotte turned pale as she listened.

"Poor Molly! poor, dear Molly!" she said;
" she has looked so anxious lately that I fear she
has not been without suspicion of coming trouble.

What a shame it seems that people who have
lived so wisely and so simply should have
trouble of this kind ! "

"Can't be helped, my dear; it would have
been just the same if Harry and Molly had
taken all the comfort of their means, for they
are not the people to save anything out of the
wreck."

"Oh dear, I do wish Molly had consented to
have the pony carriage Harry wanted to buy
her."

"If I know Molly she will be glad she did
not," said Mr. Welles; "it would make no difference to the result, but she will take comfort
that she denied herself the luxury. If, as you
think, she has seen the blow coming, it may be
better, for it will fall less suddenly; and after
all," he said more cheerfully, seeing his wife's
pained face, "it may all blow over, and if it
does I hope Harry will put a stop to his father's
folly without scruple."

But alas for our friends ! The storm did not
blow over — Bishop, Whitehead & Bishop failed;
and then it was that Molly learned what Harry
had hoped it might never be necessary for her
to know, the terrible load of anxiety he had had
to bear, and the efforts he had been called upon
to make to avert the catastrophe, if possible, or
be ready to meet it if it must come; but a folly

greater than even he could foresee or anticipate had brought all his efforts to nothing. He knew that he had himself greatly to blame, for if ·he had persuaded Mr. Whitehead to join him they might perhaps have deprived the head of the firm of the power to ruin them; but what son could so act against his father? who, after all, exhibited no other trace of softening of the brain than his loss of business judgment, and a total reversal of all his former business methods, and adoption of those which, after all, were the methods of many men in full possession of their wits.

He had not been able to bring himself to depose his father in this way. He had written to his mother to exercise her influence, but she wrote back that Mr. Bishop resented any interference in his business, and he would neither tell her anything nor listen to her.

Harry then wrote to his father entreating him to return to New York, alleging that he could not possibly manage without him; but Mr. Bishop was obstinate if nothing else, and told his son he must call Whitehead to his aid. Mr. Whitehead's father had at one time been the mainstay of the business. His son gave very little more than his name; he was generally away with his yacht, and no one would have spurned the idea of his being of any utility in the business more readily than Mr. Bishop when his mind was in its normal condition.

As not unfrequently happens, after the blow had fallen and ruin could no longer be averted, Harry Bishop seemed easier in mind. He had broken the bad news to Molly, and had found her, as he knew he would, brave and sympathetic, only reproaching him that he had kept his anxieties from her.

"You must promise, Harry, never to do that again. No matter what dreadful thing you fear, nothing can be so dreadful to me as to be left out of your confidence."

"It was for your sake, Molly dear."

"I know, but it saved me nothing; I worried just as much, for I knew you were in trouble."

"Well, dear, I promise I will share all trouble with you in future; but we hope that the worst has happened, for another year such as the last would make an old man of me."

But that night he slept profoundly, the first time in months.

Poor Molly! Poor Harry!

Of course nothing but the fact that the firm had failed was known for a few days. Not even Harry could tell whether anything could honorably be saved from the wreck or not. He worked harder than ever, staying at the office till very late, coming home on the owl train three or four times a week.

Molly tried to hope that as soon as he could settle up affairs he would have no difficulty in finding a position as bookkeeper in some large firm. He himself expressed no anxiety on that account, but he was very much troubled, when he had time to think of anything, about the future of his father and mother. How would they live? His mother had no idea of the possibility of doing without anything that money could buy.

One morning he came down to breakfast looking rather more rested than usual. He stooped and lifted little John who had toddled forward with Meg for the morning greeting. He put him down suddenly without the expected toss and kiss, and the boy's big blue eyes gazed wondering at his father. But Harry had uttered a slight exclamation of pain that attracted Molly's attention.

"What is the matter, Harry?"

"Oh, nothing," he said, smiling; "what you women call a 'stitch,' I suppose, only it is in my shoulder." He put his hand just below the collar-bone to indicate the spot, and said cheerily: "It's too sharp to last; pour out coffee, Molly, for I must not lose my train, and this pain hindered my shaving. Don't be uneasy, dear, it is too sudden to be anything but muscular."

Molly handed his coffee and he broke his egg,

but the pain increased every second; every breath he drew went like a knife through his lungs.

"Dear Harry, let me send for Doctor Price."

"But, my dear, I am quite well! I felt in unusually good spirits when I got up."

But every breath was pain, and Molly said nothing but slipped from the room and returned in five minutes with a mustard plaster. Harry still sat with his egg chipped but untouched; his coffee he had partly drank, but he was listening with his usual good-natured smile to Meg's grave prattle. His hand was held to his shoulder. He laughed when he saw Molly with her warm plate and the poultice upon it.

"You are determined I am to be an invalid, dear. I am sorry to disappoint you, but I cannot help it. I have lost this train, I suppose, but I really must take the next."

"Very well, but you have half an hour at home; now let me put the poultice on, it cannot do any harm, and may, if the pain is rheumatism, cure you. You can eat your breakfast meanwhile, and I will prepare some cotton batting to prevent your taking cold if you must go to the office to-day."

"Must go! my dear Molly, I *must* go, if I have to be carried there, to-day of all days; but I will have the plaster if you say I must."

He was so well, so unconscious of other ailment, although evidently suffering, that Molly's fears began to subside. It must be something as purely local as toothache.

But when the time came to start for the next train, Harry was on the lounge, the mustard plaster had not reddened the skin, and the pain was still sharper with every breath he drew.

"Now, Harry, I will send for Doctor Price."

"Yes, do. He must give me something or other to kill this, and get me down town to-day."

Molly flew to the kitchen and told Marta to run for the doctor. She had taken the precaution to bid her be ready before. When she returned to the parlor Harry had changed considerably.

"Give me a blanket, Molly, I am shivering, yet it is not cold," he said, as she entered.

Molly knew the chill meant illness, but she said not a word. She covered Harry up, went out and sent Anna up to prepare the bed for Harry, looked to the rubber hot-water bottle, and then returned to the children. To Meg she had given her oatmeal and milk as soon as her father's coffee was passed, and John had been given a crust of bread until Anna should be ready to attend to him; but the unexpected surprise had scared Anna and Molly so that little Johnny's breakfast was forgotten, yet he sat with perfect contentment, mumbling his crust. The moment he saw his own porridge, however, down the crust went, and he reached and jabbered for his breakfast. Molly quietly fed him, her heart heavier than lead, her eyes filling in spite of every effort at self-control. Stealthily she brushed the tears away, for fear Meg might see them and exclaim, and Harry must not guess her anxiety.

When the doctor arrived she sent the children away, and then stood behind Harry's head that she might watch the doctor's face unseen by her husband.

But it revealed little. He asked if he had taken cold? " No." Had he been conscious of cough, or oppression of the chest? " No."

Harry answered the questions readily, assured the doctor that now the chill was over he felt well, quite well enough to go to New York, if only he could give him something to numb the pain. The doctor laughed. " My dear fellow, you must not think of going out of the house to-day. It will be lucky if by care to-day you can go to-morrow."

" Nonsense, doctor! That 's all very well, but you have to pull me up; give me a hypodermic or something for this neuralgia, for I suppose that is what it is."

Molly looked eagerly at Doctor Price. If it should only be neuralgia! but his face betrayed nothing.

" Mr. Bishop, you cannot go to New York to-day ; I absolutely forbid it. You must go to bed and take the medicine I leave. We will renew that plaster with one that I will mix myself, and in the afternoon I will see you again."

Harry protested, but perhaps it was fortunate that the pain in his lung enforced the doctor's words. He recognized that he could speak only between gasps of pain.

" Doctor, doctor, can you do nothing to enable me to go to-day? I could better stay away all next week than to-day ! "

There was a look of desperate anxiety in his face as he listened to the doctor's assurances that he would not answer for the consequences should he persist in leaving the house. " I am much mistaken if you would not find yourself forced to return home on the next train if you went ! "

There was no gainsaying this. Harry hastily wrote two telegrams, then suffered himself to be put to bed.

Molly had heard the doctor say he would return in the afternoon as if it were a knell. She knew he feared something very serious.

" What do you think is the matter ? "

" I can't say just yet; I fear pneumonia, but " —

At the dreaded word " pneumonia " Molly

uttered an exclamation, although she had been prepared for it.

"Oh, doctor, that is such a terrible thing! and he is so worried!"

"Yes, that is really the serious part. His mind ought to be kept very quiet, but as I say, I still hope the pain may be only muscular; he has as yet no fever, and seems so well that I hope for the best."

But by the afternoon the fever and a cough had come. Then the dreaded pneumonia was declared in its most serious form. A second physician was called in consultation and every expedient resorted to, but there was no hope from the first. His worn-out mental condition, that had conduced to the disease, prevented any hope of recovery, and in three days Molly Bishop was a widow.

CHAPTER IX.

MOLLY'S THIRD BABY. — WAYS AND MEANS.

MOLLY was a widow! The phrase is pregnant with sadness even when the widow has less to regret in the loss of her husband, even when there is no loss of home and support connected with the grief. But to Molly, for weeks there were no degrees of sorrow; nothing could have made it lighter, no accumulation of trouble have deepened it. Harry had been everything to her, without him the sun seemed gone from the world. Only by degrees did she realize that in Meg and little John she had blessings to which she must look for alleviation to her grief; that she must brace herself to meet the future, dark as it was, for their sakes — theirs and one other than theirs; for three months later Molly's third child was born. During these three terrible months, those who loved Molly were in sad anxiety as to her future, and she herself had been forced to rouse to speak and think of business. Yet she had not begun to form plans, had not known, in fact, whether certain hopes Harry had

had of securing something from the wreck when all assets were realized were well founded or not. She had felt it impossible to go into the question, but others cherished no illusions.

Bishop, Whitehead & Bishop had come to utter ruin. There would not be a dollar. Fortunately for Mrs. Bishop, senior, the large, handsome house that had been the home of the Bishops was her own. But Molly's house was part of the Bishop estate, and would have to be given up. Neither this nor any sad fact that could be hidden from her was allowed to trouble her until after the birth of the poor posthumous baby.

Unfortunately this baby, brought into the world under miserable auspices, was a very different child from Meg or John. Molly, in addition to a mother's joys, which alone had been hers so far, without any of the weary vigils that make infancy so often a health-breaking period for the mother, now knew what it was to try vainly to soothe a restless infant.

It was not sickly, but very nervous and wakeful. And when it was but a few weeks old, Molly found she could not nurse it. All this served to rouse her from the apathy of sorrow into which she might otherwise have drifted. And very soon, too, came that other stern necessity that seems so often the aggravation of our grief, but which is generally a hidden blessing; I mean the necessity of looking poverty in the face and devising ways and means to avert it.

Something Molly must do for the support of herself and children. At the first glance, it seemed as if so bright a woman could have no difficulty. She could do several things well, and one unusually well.

"You must write," said Mrs. Lennox. "My husband has always said if you would write just as you talk, you would make a success!"

"Oh, but," Molly had answered, "I could not write anything but a cooking-book, and I have read so much of the struggles writers have to meet with before they can earn a dollar, that although I am quite willing to believe that any one who writes on a subject with which she is thoroughly acquainted will be successful, and make money, it is not a safe staff for a woman with children to lean upon. If I had even a very narrow income just to keep starvation off, and were out of debt, I think I would risk the weary time of apprenticeship which would probably, unless I should be unusually fortunate, last some years; but I remember being told, when I had a girlish ambition to support myself by writing, that Sir Walter Scott said, 'literature is a good crutch but a bad staff,' and I chose teaching because I needed a *staff*, as I do now."

Mrs. Lennox was too practical not to see that Molly must begin to make money quickly, or the little capital she had — less than five thousand dollars — would melt away. Mrs. Welles's suggestion was that Molly should start a cooking-school. She herself had been before her marriage a lecturer on cooking in England, and was one of the first graduates from the South Kensington School of Cookery, but her career was cut short by her marriage to a wealthy American, Mr. Welles. Molly too had made cookery a study, partly from natural love for it, partly in order to economize time and money when she should have a house of her own; for she had early seen that by knowing cooking by exact methods, as taught in the cooking-schools of London and America, meals which it would take the uninstructed cook hours to prepare, and then only with worry and difficulty, could be done, and were done at every cookery demonstration, in one quarter the time.

She saw that it was the same thing as an amateur workman making a table or stool, and a carpenter doing the same. In the one case, slow, uncertain work, with alterations, vexations, and as a result a clumsy article; in the other, swift, sure work, every stroke of saw or hammer telling, and in a quarter of the time a sightly result.

She would have very little to learn to make

her capable of teaching the "dainty art" she loved, and Mrs. Welles would gladly have gone back to old times and coached her where she was lacking.

"I should love to see you well started in that career, Molly, because just what you would do is needed. You are a thinker, and beside teaching how to make this and that dish, you would teach that cooking is a profession like any other; that the adept with very little time can evolve excellent dishes out of very cheap materials, while an untrained woman would have to give hours to the same work.

"The difficulty, I think, with many who try to cook by rule of thumb is that the time they seem to require discourages them; and then, though time *is* required to make elaborate dishes, very simple ones require a great deal more *attention* than they get, although the actual *time* bestowed need be very little."

Molly would have dearly loved to choose this pursuit in preference to all others, but she was handicapped by her three children and the necessity for quick success, which she could hardly expect. If she launched herself as a teacher of cooking it would naturally take many months, perhaps years, for her to make herself known. Had she been alone in the world, with only herself to provide for, she would have taken her

chances. She would have taught cooking wherever and whenever she could have found on opportunity until she was well enough known to
start a school, and her spare time should have
been devoted to pen work.

But she had to find a home for her three children, and keep her little capital as nearly intact
as possible; therefore she had not many months
to give to making her way.

The problem before her was just this : to find
some employment for her time which would
yield a decent livelihood speedily for herself and
family ; which would not necessitate her leaving
home, and would promise enough success in the
future to enable her to educate her children.

For the same reason that Molly decided
against cooking-lessons, congenial as they would
have been to her, she had to decide against opening a school for children, — one of the things suggested. That also must be a very slow success.
Of all plans, the one that seemed most feasible
was that she should take orders for fine cooking.
This might not have very quick results, but she
knew she would be without competitors in the
making of certain articles.

Mrs. Welles, who, as her most intimate friend,
was in constant consultation with her, was very
sanguine about this plan.

"I don't see, Molly, why you should not do

very well indeed in making only a few things
that are not easily purchasable, or at least, not
of first rate quality. Why, look in London!
How many have made fortunes by making one
thing better than any one else! There are Wat-
ling's pork pies and Buzzard's pound cake and
plum puddings! Those two men have not made
a living only but a large fortune. Now why
should not superlatively good pound cake, or
veal and ham pies, etc., take here?"

"But people don't know anything of veal and
ham pies here. I think I had better decide on
something else."

"Oh! traveled people do know them; and then,
has n't every one read of Mrs. Boffin's 'Weal
and hammer,' and don't you suppose they have
wondered what it is, and wanted to taste it?
Supply creates demand, so I should not wonder
if even raised pork pies would be a success; indeed, I have no doubt there are English people
enough in the country to make them pay, only
it would require time to make them known.
Then there are German specialties that are imported here, and bring a high price; those you
could make."

"Yes," said Molly thoughtfully, "I have often thought, when I have heard educated women
casting about for means of a livelihood, that I
would find out some of the imported eatables

sold at a high price, practice till I could make
them *perfectly*, and then send them to the ex-
changes. The great thing will be to decide what
are the articles that there will be most demand
for."

"Yes, and that are not already made. The
field is wide enough. A few years ago extra
fine preserves would have been well to begin
with. The peach season is just coming, but several are doing that business and more could do
it. Now we must think of something that no one
could do but you, or some one like you who has
learned the cooking of three countries."

"And who has a friend like Charlotte to
coach me in the secrets of famous English delicacies," said Molly, with some of her old arch-
ness. Sad as the necessity seems for a widow
to be obliged to look round for a living for herself and children while her grief is yet fresh, it
was the greatest blessing to Molly. Her love
for her husband had been of the kind which
might have made her widowhood the end of her
youth and brightness, had she been left with
comfortable means. She would probably have
sunk into the apathetic performance of her
motherly duties, and into a chronic sadness in-
jurious to herself and children. But this pressing necessity of bread-winning absorbed her
thoughts; the certainty that, unless she could

do something beyond what average women could do as bread-winners, her children must sink into extreme poverty, and, worse than any other evil of poverty, must live in such a neighborhood as other people of very small means, and be exposed to the bad air and see sights and hear words that every refined woman shrinks from, even for herself, and yet which cannot be avoided in a crowded neighborhood.

Bread and milk and a garret would have had little terror for her, provided the garret were well situated. And yet how few occupations there are that enable a woman to remain at home with her children, and care for them, and yet give her money enough to live decently! Therefore something out of the beaten track of sewing or giving hourly lessons in English and French, for Molly had no other accomplishments, must be devised, and, fortunately, fine cooking, the least worked field for home occupation, was the resource she had.

Molly had dismissed Anna as soon as she was able to attend to the baby herself, for she could not afford to retain her. Nor would she have been as useful with the new baby, for Molly felt no one could deal with it but herself. In its fretful, restless moods she would undress it, lay it in flannel, and rub its little back and limbs gently with her warm hand, until it was soothed and would sleep. At other times a warm bath would have the desired effect, and Molly knew that Anna, with excellent intentions, would certainly aggravate the child's nervousness by rocking it or walking it about. Therefore, in pursuing her system of mitigating the child's restlessness by keeping it as still as possible by movements soothing to the nerves, and exceeding care and regularity, she felt that no one could be trusted but herself; and under her management the little Kate was thriving, although Dr. Price had warned her that it was a very delicate baby.

Meg and John had had the natural mother food, but poor little Kate being a "bottle baby" for the first three months, her food required watching narrowly, for it was very apt to disagree. At the end of three months Molly began to feed her with a spoon, being very anxious to wean her from the bottle; for she knew children would as readily eat from a spoon, if trained to it, at four months as at twelve. But I am anticipating matters. Having decided that to make eatables for sale must be her resource, it became a question what articles they should be.

"I tell you what, Molly! We will write a list of the articles you can make, avoiding, of course, such as most people can make for themselves or buy, and then I will go and see my friend Mrs. P. at the —— Exchange and get her advice."

The two friends then sat down and made out the following list:

> English Pigeon Pie.
> Veal and Ham Pie.
> Sausage Rolls.
> Cheese Cakes.
> Cream Cheese.
> Potted Cheese.
> Twelfth Cake.

" Now a few French things, though as a matter of fact, one can buy those much more easily than English specialties," said Mrs. Welles.

" One can buy them, but only in a stereotyped way. For instance, if a large Brioche were wanted, or large Baba or Savarin, it has to be specially ordered."

" So it has, and you make either just as well as any French woman."

The French list then was as follows:

> Baba Cakes, large or small.
> Brioche Cakes, large or small.
> Gâteau de Riz.
> Vol-au-Vent of Poultry, Sweetbreads, etc.
> Bouchées.
> Consommée.

" There are several other things one could

make," said Molly, "but one must find out what is most likely to sell."

"That *I* will do," said Mrs. Welles.

Molly did not deceive herself into thinking that a business could be built up very rapidly. It might take a year to make even very little money, and she must be prepared for delays and drawbacks. Yet there seemed nothing she could do that was sufficiently remunerative that would not take time to establish. Mary Lennox, after two years' hard work, had established her greenhouse, and was making more money than she could have made in any other way; that is to say, she was making a very comfortable living, and her business in cut flowers was now growing so rapidly that she bade fair to become quite a rich woman in a few years. But had she faltered at the hard work of the first year, or been in too great a hurry for returns, she would have failed; and alas! had she been, like so many young women, obliged to provide a home for herself or others while she worked her way, she could not have thus waited for success.

CHAPTER X.

A LETTER. MOLLY HAS A NEW IDEA.

DEAR MOLLY : — As you do not come near us in our trouble, I must write and tell you what we have decided upon, although I confess it seems to me you might have shown interest enough in us to have inquired. Of course I know you have your troubles too, but everything is comparative in this world, and to come down as I and my daughters have, from wealth and luxury to not knowing what to do for a living, is something that few people are called on to endure ; and if you have lost a husband, I have lost my son, and though you may love him much, there is no love on earth like a mother's ; and I must say I thought my son's wife would have come forward to advise her mother in her trouble, especially as you have known what it is to deal with the world while I and my daughters have not. But we have now decided on a plan which will enable us to live in a manner suitable to our tastes in one sense, however mortifying to our pride in another. If you care to come and talk it over with us we shall be glad to see you. I am naturally anxious, too, about your plans. Have you decided to let us take Meg? It must be a relief to have one child less to think of, and you know our love for the darling is as great as your own.

Your affectionate mother,

ELIZABETH BISHOP.

Molly smiled rather bitterly as she read the thoroughly characteristic letter of her mother-in-law. The latter had come to her as soon as it was certain there was nothing left from the wreck, and had asked advice of Molly as being practically acquainted with the matter of making a living; and she had offered at the same time to share her daughter-in-law's burden by taking Meg off her hands entirely. This Molly declined. She knew Mrs. Bishop meant well, and that although she was left without income she was better off than Molly, for she owned a handsome house and furniture and valuable jewels.

When they had asked Molly's advice as to what they should do she had immediately suggested the obvious resource of letting the house furnished and taking a smaller one, or a flat, and the difference in rent would, with economy, support herself and two daughters.

The suggestion, to Molly's surprise, was received in dead silence by the daughters, and with scorn by Mrs. Bishop. Of course, *that* any one could see might be done, but what she wanted was a way to preserve for her girls the position they had hitherto occupied, and to do this, they *must* remain amid decent surroundings.

Molly ventured to point out that a house that required eight servants would be a very miserable home reduced to the two they proposed retaining, and that with the rent from it they might go abroad and live with comfort.

"Oh, yes, I know what living in Paris or London would be, on a limited income. We should have to go to a cheap, shabby-genteel boarding-house, and associate with frowsy dowagers, and old maids who are too tiresome to be tolerated in their own families," said Virginia Bishop.

"Of course, you could not live expensively, but I don't think it need be so bad as that. I have known very bright and well-bred people who lived inexpensively in London and Paris."

Her words, however, had no effect, and her relations-in-law parted from her with a feeling of impatience, and the reflection that young women of her class, which meant the class educated to earn their own living, never could un-

derstand the feelings, the delicacy and sensitive-
ness of *ladies*, meaning those young ladies who
had nothing but their clothes and their pleasures to think of all their lives.

Although her first discussion had been so unsatisfactory, Molly felt that duty called her to
go and see her husband's family. She could not
imagine what the plan could be that would enable the family to live in the old home, and feared
it must be something wildly impracticable.

Her worst fears were realized when she
reached Mrs. Bishop's stately home. Mr. Bishop
was looking younger and heartier than ever; the
increasing weakness of his mind seemed com-
pensated by strength of body and of will. Poor
old fellow, he cherished the hope that he would
be " even " yet with the smart operators who
had taken him in. He talked pompously of
emerging from the passing cloud, and lamented
the next instant with tears in his eyes that his
son would not be alive to enjoy the renewed
prosperity.

" But you shall, Molly, my girl, you shall."
Molly affected to hope with him, but she felt
how fortunate it was that he had nothing in his
power to waste, or his wife and daughters would
yet be utterly penniless, for he was as obstinate
in his mental decline as he had been in his
brightest days. .

But when Molly sat down to hear her mother-in-law's plan it did not seem that he was much more mad than his wife.

" Molly, we have talked matters all over, and choked down our pride, and decided that the only way in which we can live as becomes our position is to — to receive a few people of good standing into our family."

Molly fairly gasped with surprised dismay.

" You are shocked, I see, and so were we all when we realized that there was no alternative; but some humiliation we have to suffer, and this is less than some others."

" But do you think this house could ever be made remunerative for boarders ? " asked Molly, remembering that though it was large and splendid it had only three bedrooms more than those used by the family ; that there were three parlors, a library, dining-room, and reception-room (and she soon learned that it did not enter into Mrs. Bishop's plans to make any of these into bedrooms).

" My dear Molly, you really can't judge in this case," answering her tone rather than words. " For commonplace boarders, certainly this is not a suitable house ; but do you suppose there are not families who would gladly pay liberally to live in a house kept on this footing, yet be relieved of housekeeping ?   I don't expect to have a crowd of hungry people at my table every day, but one or two nice families who would pay the same as for a suite of rooms and board at the Brunswick. Superb accommodations ought to bring superb prices."

Now Molly knew this was true, and had Mrs. Bishop or her daughters had the smallest idea of making money go as far as possible — of housekeeping in any but the most extravagant way — the plan would not have been so wild; for, it was always to be remembered, Mrs. Bishop had no rent to pay. But as it was, unless one of the daughters should develop some housekeeping talent, it did not seem possible they could escape bankruptcy; and the more they revealed their plans and impracticable views, the more certain it seemed to Molly that nothing but ruin could result.

For a moment a mad idea of offering to manage for them presented itself; the next it was abandoned. Under no circumstances could she and the Bishop family have got along smoothly; for they were impressed with the fact that Molly was very much beneath them socially, and she was thankful she did not give utterance to her good-natured thought.

She returned home very anxious for her husband's family; but a bright idea had dawned in her own mind that would help the solution of her difficulties. She must leave the dear little house where she had lived five happy years. Why should she not rent a larger one and take boarders? If they were slow in coming, her cookery orders would help out; if the latter came slowly, something would be gained by the boarders.

Molly well knew her own power of making money do its full work, and knew she could cater successfully for boarders. Her resolution was taken. She would begin at once to seek the house she needed, and get settled in it before she commenced to canvass for orders.

CHAPTER XI

MOLLY TAKES A HOUSE.

WHEN Mr. and Mrs. Bishop first went to Greenfield it was a small suburban town, just becoming known to New Yorkers for its freedom from mosquitoes and malaria, and its excellent railroad. Since that time it had grown immensely. Houses were not built fast enough for the demand, and it had been said very often by Molly herself that it was a pity some enterprising woman did not open a good boarding-house. There were one or two, always crowded, and yet which people only put up with for lack of better accommodation; and it was the same with the two country hotels, where one could predict the dinner always, and know that the variety was between "roast beef and roast lamb," and "roast lamb and roast beef."

Many people she had known since she had lived in Greenfield had wished to stay a few months, but could not do so from lack of good board. She saw at once that she might be the woman to supply the want. Her thoughts flew to a house that had been long standing empty. It had been built by an over-sanguine man, business collapsed soon after it was finished, and as it was too large for most persons seeking country homes, it had stood empty ever since, getting weather worn and shabby as such houses always do.

When first the Morgan house, as it was called, had been built it had stood alone, and although quite near enough to the depot, had then been thought out of the way. Then building began, and now it was in a well built up neighborhood of Queen Anne cottages, a large, forlorn French roofed house. The fact that it had been empty so long possibly prejudiced it, although Molly found there was less reason for surprise after making her first inquiries of the caretaker, an old Irish woman, and her husband.

Having once decided, Molly was quick to act; the very next day Mrs. Welles and herself went to look at the vacant house.

"It really seems made for a boarding-house or a school," said Charlotte, when they had seen the ten good-sized bedrooms beside the servants' room and trunk-room. "I wonder no one ever thought of it before."

"Deed an' if yez knew all about it that some as lives in it know, ye wouldn't be surprised at all," said the old woman, who followed them through the house.

"Why, what is the matter with the house?" asked Molly, quickly, much startled.

"Faith an' that's more than myself can say, but niver a day have I been well in the house, an' as for me husband, he's down wid the chills every minute."

Mrs. Welles turned round sharply.

"I wonder you stay. I understand you have been in this house for years."

"Yes, ma'am, an' it's easy saying it's a wonder we stay, but there's no rint to pay, an' the coal in winther an' all, poor people can't choose their houses. But if I was the likes o' any one that cud pay, niver a bit wud I come to this place."

"Tell me what is wrong. Is the drainage bad?"

"It's me belief it's all wrong, an' I wouldn't be doing right not to let ye know."

"Well, for instance, have you bad smells?"

"Ay, indeed, smells that'll turn yer sick at yer stomach."

This was serious, and Molly was afraid she must give up all idea of such a house; yet when she had been in the kitchen and seen the condition in which the sink was, she thought it would be wonderful if there were no smells, and a further visit to the cellar confirmed this idea. Every kind of refuse was there stored, from the ashes (wholesome in themselves) of many fires, to garbage and old shoes and filthy rags and straw. Not a breath of air was admitted to the reeking mass, and they were glad to hurry away.

" Ill ! I wonder they have n't given typhoid to the neighborhood," said Molly. " Think of people leaving a house in such hands ! "

"If it had been simply closed, no doubt it would have been let long ago," said Mrs. Welles.

" You don't attach importance, then, to her account of its being unhealthy."

" Not a bit. Of course it is frightfully unhealthy now, and as you are to be responsible for other people's health I should have everything examined by an expert before you rent the place."

This was done; the landlord, only too glad to get a responsible tenant, was anxious to do everything required. The rent was $800 a year, and Molly knew that a house with so many bedrooms was likely to be profitable at that rent. The difficulty, she had observed, in making country boarding-houses pay was that few houses, unless built for the purpose, had sufficient bedrooms.

From the time the house was taken until it would be ready for occupation, Molly was so busily occupied that she had no time during the day to brood over her grief, and at night when work was over — the night that had been a long tearful wakefulness — her fatigue was so great, her mind so busy, that even then she could not long indulge in the luxury of woe. Her thoughts then naturally turned to her loss, her heart ached with loneliness, yet her mind was traversed by thoughts of her undertaking, the doubts and fears and calculations, and she would drop asleep and sleep soundly.

In work, she, like so many others, found the blessed panacea for trouble.

Of course, she had to buy more furniture than had sufficed for the little house, although she by no means intended to furnish all the bedrooms except as she found need for them.

She decided to furnish two of the bedrooms, and bought for the purpose simple, well-made ash furniture at $29 the set of four pieces. She found now, as in furnishing her own house, that it was better to buy chairs separate, and to choose them for comfort rather than custom.

Molly called up her recollections of boarding, and all the disagreeables connected with it, and determined, so far as she could help it, that those who boarded with her should have no such cause of annoyance. One she remembered was the fact that some drawers would not open without great exertion, and others would not close.

How often had she had her patience taxed by trying to get a bureau drawer exactly in the position in which it would shut. This she guarded against by testing them all, and taking such suits as were guaranteed of well-seasoned wood.

In her quest for furniture, she sought the best value for her money, but she did not look for the impossibly cheap, knowing it would be dear in the end, and very few dollars made the difference between *plain*, well-made articles and poorly made. The great difference lay in stylish furniture. Ill-made stylish, *alias* showy furniture, cost nearly double of that she bought, and yet had the prices been the same she preferred her own.

She bought squares of ingrain carpet of good quality and artistic patterns, but she eschewed dull colors, because she had no bright-covered furniture to be shown up by the neutral tint, and the whole color and brightness of the room would depend on the carpet, inartistic as such a fact might be; so she chose mingled blue and tan and, with an eye to the future making of two worn carpets into one good one, she bought both alike.

The kitchen utensils had, of course, to be on a larger scale than in her own house, but the purchase of a few large pots and pans was all she ventured upon until she should see how her venture succeeded.

Then there was extra linen to provide. All this occupied her spare time. Little Kate's restlessness made this very much less than it might have been, for though Molly pursued the plan of feeding the baby regularly and laying her down to sleep, and found no difficulty because the child had known no other way, yet the naps were very short, and excellent as Marta was, trying to do her own work and as much of what Annie had done as possible, she could not help much with the little Kate. The mother-touch seemed the only one that soothed her. This undoubtedly came from the fact that Molly, feeling that this baby was Harry's last legacy to her, had persisted in doing everything for it herself. She could not bear it away from her. Dear as Meg and John were to her, this little one seemed to need her care so very much more than they had ever done; and so the little one had developed the tyranny of helpless babyhood, and Molly found herself at last the willing slave of little Kate. But somehow it seemed as if all the care and love she lavished on it was given to its father, and so Molly had one spoiled baby.

Thus her time was very fully occupied, in those last days in the little home she had loved so dearly, and then came the sad packing-up, the final wrench with the happy past, and Molly took possession of the great house, so unlike anything she would have chosen except from a business point of view.

John and Meg were wild with delight as they scampered through the echoing corridors and rooms, laughing to hear their own voices sound so strangely.

The tears welled into Molly's eyes when she saw the glee of the children in their new surroundings, and yet she would not have had it otherwise if she could.

She had many helping hands in everything she needed to do, and very soon order came out of chaos, and the house began to seem more like a possible home.

CHAPTER XII.

MOLLY IN HER NEW HOUSE. — BEGINNING BUSINESS.

MRS. WELLES had not been idle while Molly was preparing for the change in her life. She had visited the Exchange, seen the manager of the household department, and learned from her that they would welcome *any novelties*, and especially such as would be suitable for Sunday afternoon tea.

"And that, my dear, is where I think your pigeon pies and 'weal and hammer' will come in, beside other things that you will be able to make, once your articles are known to be reliable. At any rate, whenever you are ready to send anything they will welcome it."

Molly had advertised as soon as she was settled, and she also made known as widely as possible her intention of taking boarders. Now, after careful consideration as to what would be the best article to send with a pigeon pie, she decided, as she would have pastry, to make Banbury cakes, as they are often heard of and read of, but little known.

She knew that it was more than likely her first pie might be a dead loss, for it might not sell, although Charlotte Welles pooh-poohed the idea.

"No fear, my dear, of anything so attractive looking as one of your pigeon pies remaining unsold."

"There's one thing: if I only have boarders, I shall make things that will keep a few days, and have a regular day for getting back unsold articles and delivering fresh ones; and then, as those unsold will not be stale, we can eat them at home."

Molly found, when it became known in Greenfield that she would make articles to order, that the news was received with delight; for many people sent to New York for things that they could not obtain at the local bakery, and to be able to order them right at hand, — "what a comfort that would be!"

Molly was glad to find there was this prospect, and her own common sense told her if she could produce articles not only as good to eat, but as delightful to look at, as anything supplied by the French or Italian caterers, she would get custom; but she knew the world too well to be over sanguine. She thought that what seemed so convenient now might cease to seem so when the time came, and that many would decide if they had to send to New York for wines or ices, they

might as well scud for all. Time alone could
show.

The first Thursday that she was settled, she
made the pigeon pie and Banbury cakes. She
found a farmer who kept pigeons, and from him
bought a pair for forty cents, deciding in her
own mind, that if she had to buy them often,
she would send to Fulton market and get them
by the dozen; but for this experiment the most
expensive way would be to buy too much of anything.

Molly first put a small chopping-bowl and the
chopping-knife in the ice-box to get cold while
she prepared the birds. The rolling-pin was also
placed there, and the pastry-board laid over the
top to get as cold as it would; for it was a mild
fall morning, and she needed every aid that ice
would give in order to have the pastry in perfection.

Next she put two eggs to boil hard, and then
proceeded to prepare the meat and birds, so as
to have nothing of the kind to touch when the
pastry was on hand.

She had been very particular, in choosing the
steak, to take one that was bright red in color
and of fine grain, from which the red blood
seemed ready to ooze on pressure, for this is the
sign of a *juicy* steak when cut from the round.

The dish she intended for the pie was a deep

oval holding a quart, — what English people call a pie-dish, but used here as an uncovered vegetable-dish; it had a lip all round half an inch wide, and this lip was essential to the appearance of the pie.

The steak was more than she needed to put in a pie, as the dish would not comfortably hold more than the two birds and three quarters of a pound of steak, but she needed a little meat for extra gravy. She trimmed away every bit of skin and gristle; there was scarcely any fat, for the steak was from the centre of the round before the broad band of fat was reached, which comes after the finest steaks are cut. She then cut off about a quarter of a pound of meat and chopped it with the trimmings, put it on in a small saucepan with a pint of water and half a teaspoonful of salt; this was to simmer gently all day, and at night would yield a gill of strong gravy.

This done, she laid the steak on a meat-board and hacked it all over very finely with a heavy knife, then went over it the reverse way so that it was ultimately crossed in all directions with the knife. This she now laid in the dish and sprinkled over it a small teaspoonful of salt and half a level saltspoonful of pepper. Then she prepared the birds by cutting off the head and neck and splitting them down the back. She removed the inside, reserving hearts and livers. The feet were carefully laid aside; the heads, hearts, and livers were washed and added to the gravy she was making.

The birds were nicely washed, split lengthwise down the breast, and then sprinkled with pepper and salt and laid in the dish, bone side downward. The four half birds were disposed as smoothly as possible, so that when the crust should go on, there should be as little protuberance as possible. She pressed her two hands along each side of the dish to round the contents up toward the centre into a dome. Then she took the shells from the hard eggs which she had put in cold water, after they had boiled fast for twelve minutes.

Each egg was cut in four quarters, and the pieces inserted wherever there was a hollow spot. The dish was then half filled with water and put aside while the pastry was made.

Into the cold chopping-bowl twelve ounces of flour was carefully weighed, and then a tablespoonful of it put into the dredger to use in flouring the board. Nine ounces of firm butter was also weighed and put to the flour, then chopped as quickly as possible at an open window. When the butter was about as small as hazel-nuts, a hole was made in the centre of the flour and the yolk of an egg, a small saltspoonful of salt and a scant teaspoonful of lemon juice put into it, and a gill of ice water. With her two fingers (in order that as little warmth from her hand as possible might be communicated to the paste) she stirred the water, egg, etc., and then gradually took in the flour, until she found the water all absorbed, adding more, a few drops at a time, until it formed a stiff paste. She was careful not to knead or work the paste, using only enough pressure to make it cohere. Had a novice seen the rough, ragged piece of dough, with bits of butter lying loose, that she turned out of the bowl on to the board, the novice would undoubtedly have felt that she must be making a mistake, that the dough must be made smooth ; but Molly had made it often, and had had too many compliments paid to her pastry not to feel very sure of herself, so long as she could work quickly enough to prevent those bits of butter getting soft. Once the butter melts in pastry before it gets in the oven there is an end to fine pastry for that occasion.

Molly just worked the dough enough to make it a compact but not smooth mass. Then she floured the rolling-pin (left in the ice-box till the last minute), and rolled out the paste once to half an inch thick, gathered up the crumbs of butter, etc., and put them on the dough, dredged it very lightly with flour, and folded it over one

third, then lapped the other third over that, thus
making a book-shaped piece of paste. This she
turned half round, thus bringing the rough edges
toward her. She rolled it out again, always taking care not to let the rolling-pin go beyond the
paste.

It had now formed a smooth sheet, but Molly
saw it was fast softening, and decided as this
pastry must do her credit, to put it on the ice
for half an hour. She could find plenty of
things to do while it chilled again. She therefore dredged just a dust of flour over it, and
folded it in three as she had done before, taking
great care that it was even, laid it on a tin
plate, and put it quite on the ice.

Apropos of the right and wrong way of rolling
paste, Molly's experience in teaching several
persons how to use her recipe so that a paste,
second only to the finest puff paste, and far better than puff paste as made in most private
houses should be the result, was, that the ladies
did not at all understand cause and effect. In
their hands it usually made a rich short paste.
One lady did not hesitate to say that she
thought Molly had some secret of her own, some
little wrinkle that she concealed, which caused
her pastry made in so simple a way to rise as
high as the lightest puff paste. This lady, Molly
told to bring her own materials, and then set her

to work under her direction. She found that she would have patted and smoothed the paste into shape, with her warm hand, before rolling, and that when she did roll, the rolling-pin went over the edge of the paste at each end. This tapered it off to the thickness of paper, beside squeezing all the air *out*, which it is the great desideratum to keep *in*. Nor could Molly make her see that it could matter, even when she rolled for her, and showed how the rolling-pin should stop exactly at the end of the paste, leaving it just the same thickness at the edge as any-where else.

Another lady who said her paste was dry and not a bit like Molly's, she found understood her directions to dredge a *little* flour, to mean scattering a thick layer, nearly a tablespoonful, over it, instead of, perhaps, half a teaspoonful or less from the dredger; and when the pastry stuck to the board, instead of taking it as a sign that the butter was melting, and it needed to go on the ice, the paste was scraped up, and flour thickly strewn over to prevent it sticking. To this lady, Molly explained that every abrasion of the paste must be avoided, just as if it were a skin; that should it stick, it must be gently lifted by laying it over the rolling-pin, as lifting it with the hands, unless you are very used to handling paste, will pull it out of shape or stretch

it, both ruinous to it.   But Molly felt that these
tiny points, which were the only secrets she held,
were not considered sufficient to account for her
conjuring puff paste out of what they considered
a recipe for ordinary " chopped paste " which
they had long used.

Molly found so many things to do (for in
order to work freely Marta had been sent out
with the children, and her work Molly could go
on with while waiting for the pastry to chill),
that it was some time longer than she intended
before she got back to it; but this was all the
better for her pastry, as she well knew.

When she began to roll it again, it was quite
firm, and neither stuck to board or to rolling-
pin.   She worked as rapidly as possible, rolled
the paste out to half an inch in thickness, folded
it in three again, then repeated the process, then
rolled it out ready to use.   It was about half an
inch thick.   She wet the lips of the pie dish, cut
two strips of paste an inch wide and laid round
it, pressing the inner edge, or the one next to the
meat, closely to the dish with her thumb, thin-
ning it until it went a little down the inside of
the dish.   The outer edge she was careful to
leave untouched even by the lightest pressure.
She next wet the surface of the paste slightly
with a brush she kept for pastry purposes, and
then cutting off the paste for the cover she laid it

over the meat. It was amply large to allow for
shrinkage in the oven. With both hands she
encircled what may be called the dome of the
pie, pressing the paste with the lower part of the
palm, and both making it adhere to the under
paste and also keeping the groove. The same was
done at the end of the dish, but the pressure was
only for a second; not a moment was lost, so that
the paste might not get soft. Then Molly took
the dish up in her hand and trimmed away the
overhanging paste with a *sharp* knife slanting
outwards, that is to say, in a direction that left
the edge of the paste quite flush with the dish.
She quickly laid the rest of the paste, trimmings,
etc., on the tin dish, keeping back a small piece,
then hurried with it to the ice, and returned to
finish the pie. She rolled the piece of pastry
quite thin, cut four small leaves with a pastry-
cutter from it, cut a hole in the centre of the pie,
laid the four leaves round it stems toward the
centre, rolled the paste still thinner, as thin as
paper, floured it very lightly, then doubled it up
as she would have folded a handkerchief till it
formed a little inch and a half square. She
took the four corners and gathered them together
like a bundle, making a sort of a stem of them,
then with her sharp knife she cut a deep cross
on the top. The paste could now be folded back
in some semblance of a rose, the petals formed

of the fold on fold of paste. This was inserted in the hole in the centre of the pie, and then the yolk of an egg was beaten with a tablespoonful of water, and the whole pie brushed over or glazed with it. The edges were of course untouched, as the egg would have stuck the leaves of paste together and prevented the rising. Two small slits were then made in the groove that surrounded the pie, and it was put in the oven, which was what would be called a good bread oven, hot enough to raise the crust, yet not hot enough to burn it in less than an hour. This she tested by holding her hand in it till she could count twenty-five, when she had to withdraw it.

When the pie was in the oven she took the little pigeon feet, put them in a cup, poured boiling water over them, and then quickly stripped the outer skin from them, bent back each nail until it came off, and the feet remained a vivid scarlet. This has to be quickly done, or the water will cook the outer skin, and with it will come the inner, spoiling the feet for the purpose.

When the pie had been in for half an hour, Molly turned it, and at the same time she inserted two of the feet in the slit she had made at each end of the pie, so that the little red claws stood out of it and served to indicate the nature of the contents.

Usually the feet are put in when the pie goes into the oven, but Molly found they often came out as brown as the crust, while they should be red; and when the pie was cooked, at the end of an hour, they were still red enough to be very certainly pigeon feet. Later, she removed the pastry rose in the centre, poured the gravy she had made through a funnel, replaced the " rose," and the pie was ready. It was baked a beautiful golden brown, and looked far too tempting not to find a buyer.

CHAPTER XIII

It will be remembered that Molly put the
remains of her pastry on the ice while she finished the pie. She had other work to do, and,
wishing to give the pastry as long a time on the
ice as possible, she arranged the fire so that the
oven might last well, and was just quitting the
kitchen, when there came a ring at the front
door. Molly's friends always opened the door
for themselves, and formal callers would hardly
come before eleven in the day; so it must be a
stranger. Fortunately Molly was always neat;
it was one of the blessings that she had learned
in cooking-school days that cooking did not necessitate soiling one's clothes. To be sure, she
had never reached the dainty precision of that
lady pioneer of cooking-schools in this country,
who cooked an elaborate dinner in a handsome
gown *without an apron*, doing all the drudgery,
the cleansing of birds, the paring of vegetables,
and making pastry, without soiling her cuffs or

her hands below the second joint. This was an
artistic feat, however, to which few, without
special gifts of deftness and very great practice, could attain ; but a debt of gratitude is due
to her who so completely divested cookery of its
aspect of drudgery, and proved that a woman
might, if she be only artist enough, prepare an
elaborate dinner, and have only to wash her
hands to be ready for the drawing-room. To
this perfection Molly had not attained, though
she could, and did, wear a nice dress ; but she
did not dispense with the apron, and the signs
upon it, after a day's wear, showed her that it was
necessary. She took off her apron, therefore,
and opened the door. A hack stood in front,
and a lady, unknown to her, was at the door.

"Mrs. Bishop, I suppose ! I heard that you
were going to take boarders, and came to see
you about rooms for myself, husband, and little
boy."

Molly was new to her business, and only uttered what she felt to be very inadequate :

"Yes ; I have rooms, which I will show you."

The two rooms that Molly had prepared were
shown and approved, the terms were asked, and
the current Greenfield price for each person, ten
dollars per week, was named.

"But my little boy, of course, will be half
price ? "

Now this was a point which Molly had thought over as a contingency. She knew it was quite customary to pay half price for children; yet she could not give one of the best rooms in the house to a child for five dollars a week. Even one adult would have had a smaller room, but the two she had shown were communicating rooms.

"Yes. The price is five dollars for the child; but, of course, he must then have a smaller room. I could not give a room I may need for a married couple for that price."

"Ah! that would never do, unless the room opened from mine. He is too old to need a nurse, but not old enough to sleep away from us in a strange house."

"I can show you two other communicating rooms — one large and a small one off it. The furniture is not in them, but can easily be transferred; that is, the furniture of one room. The little room, of course, could not have so large a set. I would put in it a cot bedstead, washstand, and a small bureau."

The lady, who gave her name as Tomes, was taken to see the two rooms, and did not like them nearly so well. They were equally pleasant, — the same aspect, — but Molly could see that, having seen and liked the other two, Mrs. Tomes could not take to the idea of the second

room being so small. Molly was sure she ought
not to let one of her best rooms go for a child's
use at five dollars a week.

" And you will not let me have the two rooms
you showed me for twenty-five dollars ? "

Molly rapidly thought: " It is a hundred
dollars a month ! " It was certainly very nice
to be sure of that sum; yet why should Mrs.
Tomes refuse to take the other two rooms? The
small one — ten feet by ten — was as large as
she would find anywhere for five dollars ! However, they were three, and it would be for the
winter ; and she thought it might be wise to
compromise.

" Are you willing to pay twenty-eight dollars
for those rooms ? " asked Molly.

" I think we must limit ourselves to twenty-
five dollars," was the reply.

Mrs. Tomes then arose, and there was nothing to do but to accept her terms or say " Good-
day," and Molly did the latter, but not without
a feeling of trepidation, for she feared she might
regret it; and then, again, there was some little
resentment that Mrs. Tomes should require a
first-class room for her child for five dollars a
week, and refuse to take any other.

Molly returned to her work, and later to the
kitchen to make Banbury cakes.

Molly knew the mixture for the inside of Banbury cakes would keep; so although she needed very little for use now, she made a small jar, thus: Half a pound of currants, four ounces of candied citron, four ounces of candied lemon-peel (cut very small), the grated rind of one orange, half a pound of honey, one teaspoonful of cinnamon, one-half teaspoonful of cloves, and one-half teaspoonful of allspice (all ground). The whole she mixed with a large wineglassful of brandy. The mixture was now like stiff mincemeat. (If it is thinner than this, use less honey.)

Molly rolled out the paste, laying the trimmings, which were now cold and firm, in a heap — all large pieces one upon the other, so far as possible, but not rolled up into a ball, as is frequently done with trimmings. When it was a quarter of an inch thick, she cut it with a sharp knife into circles four inches across, using a bowl of that size, turned on the paste, as a guide. Along the centre of each circle she laid two teaspoonfuls of the mixture, then folded over one side nearly one third, wet the upper surface with the white of an egg, folded over the other side, and lapped the ends again to make a sort of pointed oval; then, having satisfied herself that the juice could not escape, she turned it over on to a flat baking tin, gently flattened it with her hand, cut several tiny slits

along the middle with scissors, brushed it with
the white of an egg, and then sifted powdered
sugar over it. She made six and then baked
them twenty minutes in a moderate oven.

Molly's recollection of true Banbury cakes as
they were sold in London and brought to the
car-windows at Banbury Station, on an ever-to-
be-rejoiced-in journey to Devonshire, was that
they were a very pale yellow, covered with a
sugary icing. She was very anxious that these
should look exactly like the veritable Banbury
cakes of the London pastry cooks. But she
feared her oven, even if cool enough to bake
them as light in color, might be too cool to
make the pastry rise ; so, after they were put at
the bottom of the oven, she placed on the upper
grating a large, empty dipping-pan. This would
prevent them getting brown, while they would
cook as well.

Success rewarded her management ; for the
cakes certainly looked exactly the delicate pale
tint (yet not at all underdone) she wanted to
see them.

She had scarcely finished and taken from the
oven a pastry cake for John and Meg, when
Mrs. Welles's basket-carriage drove to the door,
with the two children and her own Lois in it.
She had picked them up and taken them for a
long drive.

Molly was glad to see her, for she was still a good deal excited about Mrs. Tomes's visit, and very fearful that she had made a mistake in refusing the offer made for her rooms, but she was reassured by Mrs. Welles's scornful rejection of the idea.

"Give a second room — and such a room! — for five dollars a week! Do you think any one in Greenfield will do it? No, my dear. I am glad you had the courage to refuse. I think if Mrs. Tomes had seen the small and large rooms first she would not have expected it."

"But some people do take boarders for eight dollars in winter," said Molly.

"Yes; but they give a winter table, and that is not what you will do, my dear. Suppose you or I needed board, do you think we could get a large room for ten dollars a week? It is only two persons who do that, and to give such a room for half ten dollars would not help to pay your bills, Molly. Wait awhile. I don't think you will be long finding your first boarder, and that will lead to others."

As if to prove her a true prophet, the same day brought a letter from a young married couple, asking terms. Molly knew something of Mr. and Mrs. Foy, and was glad to think that she might have them in her house.

She answered at once and told them all particulars. She was pretty certain that they would come, for young Mrs. Foy had often before her marriage been a guest at Molly's, and knew the kind of board she would have.

CHAPTER XIV.

MOLLY GOES TO THE WOMAN'S EXCHANGE.

MOLLY thought it would be better for her to take her wares to the Exchange herself, at least for the first time. It would be too expensive, as a general thing, to trust to others, unless her dealings with it grew quite large; for the hint had been given by the manager that if articles arriving on Saturday morning were unpacked by the consignor, or a deputy, it was a great convenience to them and an advantage to the goods themselves, as, with the best intentions in the world, in the press of business it was often found impossible to open packages until the demand for the day was over, or they were hastily opened, and their contents laid anywhere handy, but not displayed to the best advantage. Articles sent to arrive on Friday, however, did not labor under that disadvantage.

Molly was determined that her work should lack nothing that a little sacrifice of time or money at the outset could do for her; she would look on it as an investment. A man who starts

in business has to expect a few months of out-
lay before reaping the benefit of it. If he has
no capital, he has a terrible struggle in order to
exist and meet the necessary expenses.

Something like this Molly was saying that
evening to Mrs. Lennox, who had asked her if
she thought it would pay her to spend a dollar
to take in articles that would only sell for three.
" No, not at once, of course. I suppose my
profits will be *nil* this time; but then, I am hoping to make by it in future. By the way, I
must count up my expenses, to see just how I
shall come out by charging two dollars for the
pie and seventy-five cents a dozen for the Banbury cakes."

She jotted down : —

Pigeon pie	$ .85
Currants	.05
Citron	.07
Lemon-peel (candied)	.07
Spices	.05
Orange	.02
Honey	.09
Brandy	.10

$1.30

" From the pie I have pastry enough to make
a second, or tarts, or, as I did to-day, the Banbury cakes ; so that reduces the cost of the pie,

and I suppose I ought to keep a strict account of that fact, so as to see exactly what profit I make on each article, and so learn what is the most profitable to do. I may conclude that two pigeon pies would cost only one dollar and sixty-one cents. The filling for the Banbury cakes costs forty-five cents, but it is enough for two and a half to three dozen; so I may reckon the filling costs for each cake two cents. Now, if I obtain, as I hope to do, two dollars for the pie and thirty-seven cents for the cakes, less the commission of ten per cent., I double my money and have twenty-six per cent. over."

" How is that?" asked Mrs. Lennox. " Your Banbury cakes must cost more than twelve cents."

" A fraction, because I sifted a half cent's worth of sugar over them," laughed Molly. " You are counting that I used all the forty-five cents' worth of filling; but I have enough for two dozen more cakes, at least. My profits this week will just about pay my fare."

" But, my dear, suppose you really could not afford to regard this work as an investment, but *must* have the money. Many women who are forced to go to the Exchange with their work have barely enough money to buy materials. What would you do then?"

" I don't know; only I think I should be distrustful of succeeding quickly enough, if I were in the great need that such scarcity would imply, to dare venture to await results. I mean that I should do something for which there is always a real need, instead of spending my last few cents on such an errand. I could not hope to succeed at the first attempt, and would not dare to wait."

"What do you mean by work 'for which there is always a real need'?"

Molly laughed. "Well, I should not 'hanker' to do it; but I have thought the matter all over, and I am sure if I had need of an immediate livelihood or else must beg or borrow, which last is the condition your suggested possibility presupposes, I would pocket my scruples and do any menial work."

"Molly, you can't think what you are saying."

"Yes, I have thought a great deal. I know myself, and I am sure that my pride would suffer less to do some other woman's work for her than it would to beg money, which is exactly what borrowing small sums just to get along with, without any fair prospect of being able to repay it, amounts to. Think of the scorching shame of that! and yet how many helpless women go on half starving on what they can make 'genteelly' and borrowing from long suffering friends to eke out. The sort of pride that could stoop

to that, yet reject as menial *any* employment
whatever that one could satisfactorily do, I can't
understand. Many men remain out of employment months and years, leaving their families to
starve or suffer, and borrowing every cent they
can, simply because genteel employment is lacking, while the very houses who cannot find room
for all the clerks they could get, need porters.
We women all despise the men who will not
take a spade and dig rather than degrade themselves by hanging on to friends, but forget that
it is as despicable in a woman, unless she is prevented by her children from doing any work
that comes to hand. The only woman who cannot possibly do this is the one who is bound
hand and foot with a baby or very young family.
She, poor soul, must accept help, must do only
the work she can find to do at home, but even
that, it seems to me, ought not to be lacking.
How many people do we know who complain
that they would be thankful to know of any intelligent person to sew at their own homes, but
that unless work is planned and fixed it is almost impossible to get it done rightly; and to
busy housekeepers the planning and fixing is
what they want to get rid of; if they do that
they may as well save their money and do their
work at home. There is just one woman here
who not only sews but does it *intelligently*, does

not make blunders, and charges a moderate price for good work ; but she has far more than she can do. You have to wait a month for Mrs. Gibbs to take your work. There is employment for three or four Mrs. Gibbses in Greenfield, but there is only one, and other seamstresses are often in want of work."

Mrs. Lennox sewed thoughtfully a few minutes, then said : " You surprise me by a few things you have said, and I shall have to think over them quietly ; but you don't mean to say with regard to borrowed money that if you had been left quite destitute, and some well-to-do friend, say Mrs. Welles, had offered you a sum of money to start you in business, that you would have felt humiliated in accepting it ? "

" Oh, no, indeed, I should gratefully accept help to help myself, and if I saw a good chance of repaying it should not hesitate to avail myself of such aid. That is not what I mean at all by living on borrowed money."

" I think I understand what you do mean," said Mrs. Lennox, " yet it seems to me very hard to say that one would do menial work."

" Yes, very hard, I know ; something to shrink from, and accepted only as an alternative to the worse humiliation of hanging on to gentility's skirts dishonorably. Yet it must be an artificial state of things which should make any work so repugnant, especially household work. I don't feel at all degraded by washing the dishes or taking up the ashes in my own house (although I confess I grudge the time, because it is work any one can do, while I have work no one but myself can do). Why should I elsewhere?"

"Oh, the repugnance is caused of course by the class of persons who are employed in household work. It would be the same with any business or profession if only the most ignorant, least thrifty and intelligent people went into it. Nowadays any one is good enough for household work if she is not good enough for anything else."

"Yes, that must be so, and to me the chief objection to a superior woman getting her living by housework would be the contact with uncongenial companions. But in an emergency, as one can in this country always have choice of places, I would choose one where all the work would be done by myself. I should prefer hard work alone to light work with companionship; and the opportunity of being free from uncongenial companionship would make service to me preferable to factory work. As for the nonsense talked about being made to feel one's social inferiority by a lady and not by the factory overseer, that is nonsense only understandable to those who want to keep up the fiction that tyranny of mistress to maid, and not false pride, keeps decent women from service."

"You are exceptionally fitted to make your way by keeping boarders, or by making table luxuries ; but supposing for argument's sake you were as little fitted as most women — I, for instance ! what would you have done ? "

" I hardly know. I did think whether I might not start a circulating library, we hear that one is so much needed here."

" A circulating library ! why of course ! "

CHAPTER XV.

EARLY next morning Molly started to town, taking the pie in a small wooden box that came from the grocer's and had held fine canned goods. The Banbury cakes were packed round it in waxed paper with utmost care that the glazed surface of the pastry should not be injured. The vacant space was filled with cotton batting covered with waxed paper, and then covering the box with paper she put a shawl strap round it. The package was neat enough, but by the time she reached the Exchange she found it quite sufficiently heavy.

She arrived early, found every one busy, but after unpacking the pie whose appearance bespoke favor for it, she was allowed to place it very prominently on the showcase where every customer would see it. She had a card ready prepared on which was written in large, clear characters, —

ENGLISH PIGEON PIE.

The Banbury cakes were ticketed in the same

way, and Molly told the superintendent she would call in the afternoon, and if the articles were not sold, take them home and send fresh for the next week.

When she did return in the afternoon she was quite prepared to find that her pie was still there, but that she might be encouraged to send again, and to learn from comments made that a smaller size would suit better, or even that meat pies would hardly be popular. But there was better fortune in store. The pie was sold and four of the Banbury cakes, and the manager suggested a larger supply next week, and that some kind of pie might be sent that could be cut into pieces and sold, so much a portion, for the ladies' lunch.

Molly returned elated and very hopeful, although she was too sensible to think that to-day's good fortune was anything but a lucky chance.

" And the fact, my dear, that the pastry showed for itself that it was of the puffiest; the best kind of omen for the contents, — add that to your element of good 'luck,' " interjected Mrs. Welles, as Molly related her experience. She decided to make a Windsor pie the next week, to cut, as well as a second pigeon pie, and also more Banbury cakes.

Monday brought a visit from Mrs. Foy, who engaged one of the rooms Molly had ready.

And a few days later Mrs. Tomes returned to see if the rooms she had been offered were vacant, and finding one was not she seemed much annoyed, then finally decided on taking the one shown her with small hall room for her little boy, at twenty-four dollars. It was a dollar less than the price, but Molly accepted it.

She was now beginning to keep house for herself, three children, and five boarders on forty-four dollars a week. Molly had determined when she decided to take boarders that, no matter what happened, those who paid her should have as good or better board than they could get elsewhere. Of course, once she had several boarders that would be easy enough, but she had known cases of women who had to struggle along with two or three who suffered, at least to the extent of poor food, because the small incoming went so little way toward the out-going. She knew should she have long to wait with only three or four she would have to manage very cleverly to avoid going behind, or giving poor board. One reason why, with only partly enough money coming in, many a woman is forced to ruin the reputation of her house, and lose even her few boarders, is because, too often, that amount has to provide for all her private family just the same food as for the boarders. This Molly resolved to avoid. If she intended to succeed she must make the table something that would commend itself. If this must be done only for two boarders, instead of providing for all the household alike, she would simply send in for the one or two the dinner they ought to have, having a much simpler one for herself and children, and continue to do this until there were enough boarders to enable her to have a generous table for all.

, She had been told by women who had got rich by keeping boarders that there was no profit until you had six or seven, after that every one counts ; of course under six there would be loss, and she had observed enough to know that it was while waiting for the six that many a woman fails, especially if she has five or six of her own family who are to be supported out of money paid by two or three boarders. A wise woman would keep her own family on oat-meal and milk, that her boarders might have a satisfactory table and so draw more; but instead of that too often the service is insufficient, and the food poor. These were the breakers she must steer clear of. She must also avoid in-trenching on her little reserve, or otherwise go-ing into debt. Therefore she decided to make a rough calculation of what her expenses might be expected to be, and how far the forty-four dol-lars a week would go to meet them.

CHAPTER XVI

INCOMINGS AND OUTGOINGS.

MOLLY'S income from her boarders was $44 a week, which, as there are four weeks and one third of a week in each month, would give her $190 with which to meet her monthly expenses. She sat down with pencil and paper and marked down what her expenses would be so far as she knew them for the first month, then she would know what she would have for the other expenses : Rent, $66.66 ; servants, $26 ; coals, $5 ; tea, $3 ; milk, $10 ; total, $110.66. This would give her $80 for the butcher, baker, grocer, and all the other household expenses. The second servant was an immediate necessity, and the next month the fuel must be at least doubled ; at present it was needed only for the kitchen, which did not burn more than a ton a month. Ice would not increase, and in allowing five quarts of milk a day she expected to have enough by taking it under her own charge. She had the experience of others to tell her that milk is one of the mysteries of housekeeping.

Sometimes a gallon barely seems to supply the coffee for breakfast, but when an attempt is made to see where the great leak can be by watching the pitchers, etc., the gallon seems to increase by magic and the milk is abundant. Molly, therefore, had decided to buy one of the neat refrigerators that come for dining-room use, and to keep butter, fruit, and milk under her own eye, sure that she would save money by doing so.

She did not expect with the five boarders she had to find her own expenses all paid ; to put it plainly, she did not think that she and three children and two servants could live on the profits made on five people, if those people were to have what they had a right to expect.

Molly, when she resolved to keep boarders, had called to mind all she could remember to have been told to her by those who had made a success of the business, and she well knew that the two women who had made most money gave better food and accommodation for the money than any one else. They probably were content to make less at the beginning, and when numbers increased, as there was rarely loss from long continued vacancies, they began to make a profit. And Molly could see for herself that if income from the five (or it may be said four and a half) boarders she now had went near to pay all expenses, as she would be at no extra expense with half a dozen more, except just for what they ate, she would then be clearing a handsome sum each month.

This all seemed clear as daylight, and yet when she remembered what struggles and distresses she had known women even with several boarders to endure, she could not understand; it seemed as if her own calculations must be too sanguine. True, the women of whom she was thinking lived in large cities where the rent was more than double her own; but then also for the best rooms they could and did ask much higher prices, and the smallest they would let for no less . than she would get for her best rooms.

"Well, it's no use for me to worry about what others do or cannot do; I must just do the very best I can, see that every dollar is used to the best advantage, and then try to do right."

Mr. Welles laughed when Molly gave her views of keeping boarders.

"So you want to give your boarders all you possibly can for their money, instead of as little as they will be satisfied with! There is a great deal of novelty in that idea, and I often thought a boarding-house on such principles ought to be a great success; it is one of the great business secrets."

" What is ? " asked Mrs. Welles, who was strongly against Molly giving people too much for their money, although she would almost certainly do so herself.

" The secret of the gigantic retail businesses that have grown up of late years in New York, London, and Paris, is to sell quickly at very small profits; small profits and quick returns make more money than large profits made slowly."

" Oh, bother your business maxims. Molly's returns won't be a bit quicker if she gorges her boarders on real spring chicken and tenderloin steaks and puff paste, than if she gave the usual imitation articles."

" They may not be quicker, but they are a great deal more sure. Do you suppose any one will leave when they get such fare ? and don't you suppose that there will soon be competition to get rooms here, and Mrs. Bishop may then charge fancy prices, if she likes. Just look at the matter for a moment as a business man would. Most boarding-houses change boarders often; every week or two there is a vacancy, sometimes several. Every vacancy means nearly ten dollars a week loss. That is to say, if only one or two leave when eight or ten remain, the difference in the marketing would be hardly perceptible. Each double room vacant means a loss

of twenty dollars if only empty one week, and in
an average house it may be empty longer; just
put that twenty dollars into your butcher's and
grocer's bill for the month and see what a difference it makes. Your essentials are the same,
your rent, servants, fuel, lights, because you
can't cut down your running expenses with every
variation in the number of boarders. This being the case the woman whose house is always
full could make money and give excellent board,
while the one who has frequent loss from short
vacancies will stint her boarders and yet be a
loser, and the more she stints the greater her
loss."

"So it has always seemed to me," said Molly.
"Mrs. MacIntyre, who began with a small house
in a cheap block in New York ten years ago,
and now has three houses very handsomely furnished on Madison Avenue and is fast making
money, told me her success was due to the fact
that her boarders, at least the married ones,
stayed on for years, and did not leave town in
summer till late, instead of being in a hurry, as
people less comfortable would be; and that in
order to secure their rooms for fall they often
paid room rent for summer, so that even at that
season she did better than most people. Of
course, there were exceptions. I know, too, that
where we boarded in New York, with a little care

and *no more expense* to our landlady, we might have lived much better, and the changes would have been fewer, yet it was, all things considered, a very fair house. We only paid twenty dollars a week for two, and the people who had what were called the best rooms, thirty; so I, paying less than half the city rent, ought to give very good board indeed, although I find $10 for each person is considered a very good price here, $8 being quite general, while $10 is very low for New York; I mean, of course, in decent localities."

"Cuthbert, I am ashamed of you encouraging Molly to wear herself out for other people. That is just what she is planning to do," said Mrs. Welles, as they walked home.

"Nonsense, I am encouraging her to become a successful woman, which she will do if left to herself. She has the right ideas."

"Oh, Cuthbert, what can you know about it?" asked his wife impatiently.

He laughed heartily.

"Do you think a moderately good-natured man will go through life and not be consulted by less fortunate women friends as to how to make a living? I know I have been consulted half a dozen times by the widows of business friends, and I have always found that although a teacher understands that she must teach all day in or-

der to make a living, and so does a woman who
proposes to go into any business except taking
boarders, those who in their reverses have
asked my advice about utilizing their houses for
this last purpose, I always found were looking
forward to leading almost exactly the life they had
hitherto led.   They had in their more prosperous
days kept two, perhaps three, servants, and they
proposed to go on with those and hoped to get
several inmates ; but I never met with one, except Molly, who expected actually to work herself at the beginning.   The expectation generally is to make money by giving as little time as
possible and no real work."

"Yes, but I've heard you say a dozen times,
Cuthbert, that no one can work themselves and
direct others."

"That's true enough; only when the business
has to be made a wise man works with his men,
not doing their work or helping them, but doing what they cannot do.   Mistress Molly says
she intends being her own cook until she has
experience in quantities, knows just how far
things will go, in fact, until she learns her business; and by her cooking she will make the reputation of her house.   Her rock ahead will be
that she will naturally want to employ a cook
later to relieve herself.   Where will she find a
substitute for herself ? "

" That's it ! She will spoil these people, and
then kill herself to keep up to her reputation."

Mr. Welles laughed again.

" You rave against Molly and would do exactly the same yourself."

" Of course I should, but I 'm as strong again
as Molly."

" It 's the strength in the heart, my dear, the
courage and energy, and you both have that."

CHAPTER XVII.

EXPEDIENTS AND DIFFICULTIES.

WITH regard to the laying out of the eighty dollars Molly could as yet only give a rough guess. She would be better able to tell at the month's end, but it seemed to her that it would almost pay her bills. Had the weather been cold enough to allow of her going to Fulton Market for fish and vegetables she knew she could buy to better advantage; that, however, she could not attempt to do until November, but she made an arrangement with her butcher by which, on taking a half sheep or lamb, she got it very much cheaper, because he thus got rid of the less prime parts, while Molly could use every part to advantage; and while her table was so small she arranged for him to hang the meat in his ice closet. It would be the same with beef if her family became large enough to use much soup. Her only fear was that in attempting to give a very good table she might not be able to afford the great variety some houses whose table was by no means good provided. She had a keen recollection of three kinds of roast meat, all inferior as to cooking and quality, being considered necessary in a house with twenty boarders, and in talking of it, the landlady had deprecated the necessity, saying, what was quite true, that she could not afford that the three joints should be the best of their kind, nor could one cook be expected to cook the three roasts besides a variety of vegetables *properly ;* and yet the boarders set so much value on variety that they would not be satisfied with less. If this should be true it would be a terrible stumbling block in the way, but Molly decided she would try first what simple, excellent dinners would do. She would then take care to find out what each one disliked and avoid it.

So the first night that Mr. and Mrs. Foy dined, Molly provided

Vermicelli Soup.

Roast Beef.   *Yorkshire Pudding.*

Mashed Potatoes.   *String Beans.*

Ramakins.   *Apple Pie.*

Nuts.   *Grapes.*

Coffee.

She had hoped by having dinners that required little or no attention after she herself left the kitchen that she could manage to let Marta take care of the children, and the waitress attend table, but she found this did not work.

The ramakins had been made by Molly and put in the oven, the vegetables were all cooked and dressed, but John and Meg had not been accustomed to go to bed till seven, and it was impossible to send them at six, the usual Greenfield dinner hour. Kate was bathed and laid in her cot, but Molly had to leave John and Meg with Marta who perforce was in the kitchen, and her heart was in her mouth at every sound. She pictured to herself their dear little hands grasping a saucepan handle or the hot oven door, or eluding Marta in a dozen ways, probable and improbable, and she decided she could not stand another such ordeal.

She could have managed, perhaps, better by having everything cooked and left ready for the waitress to bring in and letting Marta go upstairs with the children ; but that would be at the cost of the excellence of the dinner, which somehow Molly could not bring herself to do, so she resolved until she could afford a nurse to eat her own meals early with the children. She would then remain in the pantry to send things in, to carve, and watch any little articles still cooking in the kitchen, although she tried to avoid the last as much as possible.

The next night, therefore, when Mr. and Mrs. Tomes had joined the household, Molly sent the dinner in, and did not herself go in until the salad was put on.

She adopted this plan with great regret, and from the simple necessity of choosing between her own convenience and the comfort of her boarders. The alternative was very disagreeable to her; she felt it was a somewhat undignified position, but not for a moment must her dignity be put in the scale against her duty, and she did not yet dare to incur the expense of a third servant.

But not many days passed before Molly began to think that she had been forced into a very wise thing. She found that by carving at leisure she could do it more thoroughly and carefully than at the table. The one night she tried it, although only two were at the table, she had not known what she had eaten herself, nor had she enjoyed her meal. Now she dined at noon with the children. She found by knowing exactly what was left after the dining-room was served she could arrange for next day; and as the servants also dined in the middle of the day, what was left from the evening was all available.

To give as minute an account as I would like to do of Molly's management of her boarding-house would take treble the space that I have at command, and my story would run to the terrible dimensions of a Richardsonian novel. Some slight sketch of the kind of meals she furnished I will try to give, with a few recipes where they enabled her to make her table seem much better than the average, although the cost was no more to her.

I must not forget to say that Molly had paid careful heed to one thing Mrs. Welles had said.

"Molly, remember, you must take lessons in carving. My father would carve a turkey so that a dozen people each got a plate of meat with some of the breast. My husband, when he has cut for six people, begins to look round and wonder if the breast will hold out, and whether he will not have to break up the carcass pretty soon. While my father's turkey would leave the table a respectable bird still, Cuthbert's is a disgrace, and no one has had nice pieces."

"I know; I have observed that mystery before. One would think so many pounds of meat would only satisfy just so many people, no matter how it is cut; yet it does make the greatest difference; but how could I take lessons in carving?"

"I don't know; it's easy enough and common enough to do it in London, but I'll ask Cuthbert to find out."

The carving lessons had to lie in the future, but she did take care to have her knife like a razor, and this made a great difference. The leg of mutton carved into clean, neat slices looked very different, both on the plate and on the dish, from one hacked and torn by a bluut knife. With the roast beef it made even more difference, for the meat, being diversified with fat and lean, was less compact.

As I have said, Molly inquired of her boarders what they disliked. She found the Foys liked everything but stewed oysters or oyster soup. Mrs. Foy ate neither of these, nor did she like curry, which Molly was careful to ask, but her husband did. The Tomes did not eat veal, and disliked hash and stewed meats of any kind.

This rather upset Molly's programme; she had hoped, if her boarders would let her, to give them remarkably good meals; but if nothing but roast meat or steaks and chops would serve them she supposed they must have what they wanted.

She thought the matter over. Of course she meant to have the very best roast of some kind every day, and she must watch for a few weeks. Many people protested against things that they really liked very well. She must try to make her table as like a good *private* table as possible. Surely that must be appreciated.

Nevertheless she was careful to bear in mind the tastes of her boarders as far as possible. For instance, on days that there was oyster soup, Molly remembered a day ahead to have a plate of other soup for Mrs. Foy; a very inexpensive and easy matter when the family is large. Stewed oysters was a Sunday tea dish sometimes, then Mrs. Foy's oysters were given her on the half-shell. However, these matters belong to Molly's table management, of which details will come later.

There was one source of profit and comfort that Molly was anxious to take advantage of, and that was having the laundry work for the boarders done by a laundress hired by herself. She asked Mrs. Foy and Mrs. Tomes if they would like their washing done in the house, and they were very glad, as Molly herself when boarding had been when the chance offered.

For the first week she hired a woman who had worked for her for some time when she needed extra help, and on whose work she could depend. She came two days and a half. The price for mixed washing was seventy-five cents a dozen, and the woman's wages was $2.50. The boarders had between them three dozen pieces, and the house washing was thus done for next to nothing. Before the second week Molly had engaged a laundress at $16 a month, and as until the house was full she would not be more than half employed in the laundry she was to help in other ways.

Now Molly could have sent her children up-stairs in Delia's charge and herself presided at the table, but her present plan was of such advantage in some ways, that she would by no means change it at present.

So well had Molly's wares pleased the patrons of the Exchange that she had received a note : —

" Will you make two dozen cheese cakes, as well as more Banburys ? "

Molly had intended, it will be remembered, to make another pigeon pie, also a Windsor pie that could easily be cut into portions for lunch, and Banbury cakes, for her second week's consignment, and this order, which had come without soliciting, encouraged her very much. The pastry making enabled her at a mere nominal cost and very little more trouble to put a dainty dish of fine pastry on her table for dinner that night by making two or three extra Banburys, and the same of cheese cakes, and while making the Windsor pie she made one to eat cold for luncheon.

In making up the pie she worked exactly as for the pigeon pie, only for variety's sake instead of ornamenting with leaves she cut a small square about three inches by three, laid it on the centre of the pie, and then cut with a sharp penknife a good-sized hole through both it and the cover to let out steam. To hide the hole she made a little ornament of thin pastry many

times folded, and cut with a sharp knife into a
sort of daisy, on the principle of the pastry rose
she made for the pigeon pie; then all was
brushed over with egg carefully. (See directions for Pigeon Pie.)

Molly had early in the week had half a ham
boiled. It was nice for lunch. A thin slice of
it was often required to give a piquant flavor in
making sauce or soup, and it was now on hand
for

WINDSOR PIE. Put at the bottom of a deep,
oval pie-dish or "baker" a layer of lean, un-
cooked veal sliced half an inch thick. (Shoulder of veal is excellent for this purpose.)
Sprinkle over it a scant saltspoonful of salt and
pepper, mixed in the proportion of one saltspoonful of pepper to five of salt; then put a *thin* layer
of ham and one of forcemeat (for which the recipe will follow). Both the layer of ham and of
forcemeat must be very thin, yet ham must cover
the veal entirely, as you would cover the bread
with it for a sandwich. Then the forcemeat must
be evenly laid all over the ham, but both together
must not exceed half an inch. Now lay another
layer of veal and salt and pepper, then ham and
forcemeat again, until the dish is quite full.
Lay something flat on it, then a weight, for an
hour. Meanwhile have prepared from bones
and scraps of veal about a pint of stiff veal jelly,

very well seasoned ; pour this over the meat. Wet the lip of the dish, lay a strip of pastry all round, pressing lightly to make them adhere, then lay on the cover. (See directions for Pigeon Pie.)

Prepare the forcemeat thus : —

Half a pound of lean veal (in cold weather pork sausage meat is better and saves trouble), chop it very fine ; a cup of fine, stale bread crumbs without any crust whatever, a dessertspoonful of finely chopped parsley, a saltspoonful of finely powered thyme, savory, and marjoram, a good teaspoonful of salt, *scant* saltspoonful of pepper. Mix altogether with enough butter to make a crumbling paste.

CHAPTER XVIII

CHEESE CAKES. — COLD MEAT PIE. — COLD MEAT
FRITTERS, AND OTHER RECIPES.

CHEESE cakes were things that Molly had ex-
perimented upon considerably before finding the
recipe she liked. The old-time form called for
sweet curd, dried and sifted, and this was perfectly satisfactory to the palate, but very tiresome to do. The modern recipe, which does
away with the curd, but retains the other ingredients, she found more like lemon pie, and not
the real cheese-cake texture. Now she was well
aware that the principle on which the curd was
used was the same as that of the beef in mince
pie, — merely to afford a solid foundation for
the richer ingredients. She had, therefore, tried
bread crumbs, sponge-cake crumbs, and floury
potatoes, rice flour (boiled to a stiff mush), and
rolled cracker, and had decided on using the latter. The rice made a delicious variety, but it
was too moist for the orthodox cheese cake.
The recipe she used was as follows : —

ENGLISH CHEESE CAKES. Four   ounces   of

rolled cracker, three ounces of fine butter, yolks of two eggs, two tablespoonfuls of brandy or sherry, two ounces of sweet almonds, half an ounce of bitter almonds, beaten to paste, the grated rinds of two lemons (medium size), the juice of half a lemon, and three ounces of granulated sugar.

The butter was creamed, the cracker added, then the yolks of eggs, brandy or wine, and sugar, all beaten very well.

As in all cases of old-time recipes that called for almonds beaten, Molly used almond paste, and when bitter almond was to be a distinct flavor, as in this case, she added a few drops of almond extract. She grated the almond paste to crumbs, and beat it in with the other ingredients. When all was thoroughly mixed, Molly put the bowl aside, and proceeded to fill oval patty-pans. Of course, round cheese cakes would have been as good to eat, but not so pretty to look at ; and Molly had the instinct of business, and knew that form in pastry and cake has very much to do with their selling qualities.

When the patties were lined and pricked a little on the bottom, to prevent the pastry rising under the filling, she filled each one, and quickly put them into a hot oven. Perhaps it may be needless to say to those who have watched Molly using pastry, that the edge was only trimmed off with a sharp, steel knife. There was no smoothing with the finger; in fact, she touched the pastry as delicately as if it were white tulle, and *not one unnecessary touch was given.*

The cheese cakes took twenty minutes for the crust to be a very pale brown and the filling the color of ground cinnamon.

These were packed, when cold, with the pies, and sent to the Exchange by express, to arrive Friday night. Molly had obtained a grocery box, and, by means of a thick cardboard division, had packed therein the two pies; then laid over these a cardboard cover, which was prevented from touching the top of the pies by a layer of waxed paper, cotton, and excelsior packing, and small slats fastened with tacks along the sides to prevent the pressure (the centre division also tended to do this); then came more excelsior, and each cheese cake, wrapped in waxed paper, was laid on it, a layer of cotton wool on them, and the box was filled up with excelsior and the cover nailed on. Molly's aim in packing had been to avoid friction, which would spoil the appearance of her productions, and, as the result showed, she succeeded.

These were busy days for Molly, although she did not find herself overworked. She was too sensible to risk her health and her children's welfare by overdoing, and fortunately, although energetic, she was not nervous, and was exempt from that curse of busy-minded women — the tyranny of nervous excitement — that drives us to work long after the need has ceased. I say it drives *us*, as if women were peculiarly subject to it. Physicians, however, say that business men suffer from it quite as much. *They* are told to rest from business, but *cannot* take rest, although they know they are not needed in business ; rest is impossible, for a seeming necessity drives them back to their desks. But Molly, happily, had never known the long-continued, wearing cares that lead to this condition. She knew grief ; but worry was a stranger to her, partly because her own temperament led her to do the best she could, and what she could not attain to, to leave unaccomplished. This uncommon philosophy extended to her social life. Never had she known a pang on account of being less well off or less well dressed than her neighbors, nor would this feeling ever add a pin's weight to her burdens.

But, although not overworked, her days were well filled ; for her second servant was by no means one to be left unwatched. Molly had not dared, with new people in her house, to engage a newly-landed girl ; and yet, when she saw the result of a couple of years "in the country," she regretted that she had not risked it. Marta was as good as a girl could be, and, as she was a fair cook and devoted to the children, Molly preferred to look to her for aid with them when not busy in the kitchen, and with the help of Molly's deft hands, Marta had plenty of time to be almost as good as a nurse.

Molly's daily routine was something as follows : she wrote over-night her orders for breakfast, which Marta cooked, while Delia prepared the dining-room, did the hall work, steps, etc. Molly, immediately after her own toilet, always went down-stairs, not to do anything, but to see that all was going on well. She knew that the certainty of her presence in the kitchen at a quarter to seven o'clock would do very much to keep things going straight. Having looked around, seen that all was right, or setting it right if wrong, she went up-stairs, washed Meg and John, who were at present bathed over-night, and gave little Kate her bath. Meg, who was able to dress herself with very little aid, and help John, would "run a race with mamma," as to whether she or Kate would be dressed first. This was a very happy half-hour for Molly. The children's pranks were amusing; but, most of all, Meg's tricks to attract Molly's attention, and so hinder her that she, herself, might finish first ; and her screams of laughter when she thought she had succeeded in her tactics never failed in bringing a similar response from Molly.

The breakfast, as yet, did not include hot cakes; so that, when it was cooked, Marta could leave the kitchen and give the children their breakfast in the little room Molly had appropriated for the purpose. One of the chief objections to a family boarding she had always considered to be the injury to children from sitting at a boarding-house table, and she could not consider it would be less in her own house. Her first care, therefore, was that her children should be brought up as privately as possible, without the hurtful influences of hearing older people's talk and comments. This she meant to accomplish, and, with the assistance of her trusty Marta, she found it easy.

The breakfast consisted of some form of porridge or mush, and either muffins, corn-bread, rolls, or biscuits, and one kind of meat, either chops, liver and bacon, ham and eggs, steak, veal cutlet (when some little dish would have been prepared for Mrs. Tomes), sausages, or fish. One or other of these dishes was provided every morning. Hash, with eggs, was occasionally given for breakfast; but, because of the prejudice against this excellent dish, it was rarely introduced. Mock terrapin took its place in using up cold meat as cold weather came, and was much liked and looked upon as something very superior; it really cost no more than hash, except that it took more time to prepare it. But Molly's friends will long since have known that she had learned to look on time as money, and to coin it into money — that is to say, twenty-five cents' worth of meat and half an hour's time would be as good as fifty cents' worth of meat and ten minutes' time. As good! — how very much better? — only those who have tried can know. So cold meat and Molly's time — and not much of it, either — made mock terrapin, while the same cold meat and half the time would have made hash and a discontented house.

Potatoes, in one form or other, were always on the table, and fruit preceded the breakfast. When melons were moderate in price, Molly bought those; otherwise, as long as peaches were plentiful, she provided them. One rule she had soon laid down for herself; that was, to market exactly as she would for her own family. If peaches were dear, she would have to buy inferior steak, or less in quantity, if she put them on the table; therefore, she would have ice-cold baked apples. At first, as we have seen, Molly had thought she must give people what they expected to have; but a week's experience with Mrs. Tomes cured her of that.

Her son was eight years old, and the first morning he announced to his mother, as he ate his ice-cold peach — for it was in attention to such little matters that Molly hoped to excel; therefore, the fruit was kept on ice till the last moment — in a whisper, loud enough for all to hear: —

" I say, ma, this is a good deal better than that other plaguy old place. Hope they don't have " —

At this point, no doubt, a maternal warning had been conveyed, and Molly could only wonder what he hoped she " did not have."

Yet, notwithstanding that it was evident fruit had not formed part of their breakfast until now, Mrs. Tomes looked with a frown if baked apples were presented to her when she expected melon or peaches, and those two fruits were both too expensive at this season to buy; and also, on a perfectly broiled chop being placed before her after she had been a few days in the house, she said to the waitress : —

" Is there nothing else ? I don't care for chop."

Delia had been told in such a case to say that there was cold ham (or whatever might be the meat on hand) or eggs.

With a discontented look, Mrs. Tomes took the chop.

Now, Molly did not have twice in one week the same kind of meat, and Mrs. Tomes had expressed herself as very fond of chops and steaks — so much so that Molly had feared that it would be difficult to cater for her, for she had remarked in her experience that there are none so difficult to provide for satisfactorily as your " plain roast and boiled " people, and who like nothing but steak, chop, and roast beef.

In after years Molly, looking back on this year of effort, considered that the hardest trial she had had to bear was the discontent of people who were not satisfied to live in some one else's house as they would have done in their own; who, in fact, in their own homes, for the same money, would have lived much less luxuriously and well; yet, because they were boarding, wanted the variety of a third-class hotel, instead of appreciating the fine quality, the excellent cooking, and the small perfections of a private, well-kept house, which are almost invariably absent from the average boarding-house, and which are only attainable by unvarying attention on the part of the landlady — trifles that cost nothing, but which every boarder knows the lack of. These trifles, Molly decided, should not be neglected in her house.

" No wonder," she thought, " women who take boarders get discouraged, and care only to provide routine meals ! "

Nevertheless, Molly did not allow herself to be discouraged. This was perhaps because, although *Mrs.* Tomes was a thorn, Mr. Tomes, after they had been in the house a few weeks, expressed hearty satisfaction, and youthful Mrs. Foy, who had boarded very much before her marriage, said, as a convincing proof of her approbation : —

"I don't believe I shall ever care to keep house, Mrs. Bishop, so long as I can board with you. Mr. Foy agrees with me in thinking this is just the most home-like way of living. At least, if we keep house, we will build near, and come to you for meals, if you will let us; for I confess I do want a dear little box of a house of my own."

Molly laughed.

"If I succeed, you may do so, and one thing that will help me to succeed is just such encouraging appreciation; and I am very much obliged to you for letting me know you are satisfied."

"Satisfied! I should think we would be hard to please if we were not. But I wanted to ask you something. Mr. Foy has two friends who think they would like to come out here for the rest of the fall; but we did not know whether you would care for transient boarders."

"While my rooms stand empty, I shall be only too glad," said Molly.

They came; and it may be said here that, although they only stayed to see the last of the autumn leaves, they were so pleased that the next spring they bespoke the first vacancy Molly might have.

But all this is a digression from Molly's routine of daily work, in which we got no farther than the breakfast.

After leaving the table, Molly went to the pantry to see what had been removed from it, for she had given orders that all food left should not be taken to the kitchen until she had seen it. (For the kitchen breakfast she always made separate arrangements.) There was not often much left, for Molly satisfied herself with providing plenty without the waste of having much cold food to warm over; but on mornings when eggs were provided, there would be sometimes two or three left, and Molly knew servants well enough to be sure that any other but Marta would throw them away, and never dream of putting them to use; also, any small bit of meat would be considered not worth saving, although they would not perhaps have wasted a large piece. The eggs would boil hard for salad or other purposes. Molly would give orders what was to be done with the various things, and then would go to market — in Greenfield at present, although in colder weather she intended to go to

Fulton Market for supplies, because of the variety to be obtained there, and because she knew that in large markets there were times when certain articles, usually very dear, were quite cheap. Thus game, salmon, and choice poultry, which, when to be had at all in Greenfield, were always about a dead level in price for each season, were often to be found at prices which made them almost as cheap as butcher's meat.

It is true that Molly did not feel equal to marketing profitably at a large city market; although she was an unusually good judge of meat, poultry, and vegetables, she was a stranger to the ways of the markets, and the terms for some things differed from her own, as they do, indeed, in each city; and she decided before she undertook that phase of her housekeeping to take lessons in marketing. She might not learn much as to meat and provisions, but she would learn the ways of the place. She knew that to seem uninformed in this, as in other matters, is to lay yourself open to imposition, or to ridicule if you refuse to be imposed upon.

In her present marketing, however, she adhered to the principle which had guided her in her own housekeeping — that is, to take care that one day's expenses balance the other. For instance, she might decide to buy rather an expensive article, such as young ducks or spring chickens, which would cost beyond the limit she had laid down as her average, and if she purchased once or twice a week like this, and allowed her usual dinner bills to be up to the average on other days, she would have been a considerable loser in the end, or else had "skimpy" days; but, instead of that, the day she had been extravagant was always followed by one on which the dinner cost less than the average, as, for instance, instead of following it with roast beef, she would have braised beef or a leg of mutton. The same with desserts. Once a week or so, she would indulge in Nesselrode pudding or ice-cream bombe; but by the end of the week her expenses were balanced by her spending a little extra time and making less expensive desserts. But she often was amused to find that the dessert costing, perhaps, twenty-five to forty cents was as much enjoyed as those costing double.

Upon her return from the market, Molly, after removing her things, went through each room to see if the beds were nicely made, the ewers washed and filled, and that nothing had been neglected that ought to be done. The mere fact of Delia knowing she would do this made her more careful to neglect nothing. This daily visiting became more necessary when fires came into use. After this inspection she prepared the children to go out, and in these early days either Delia or Marta took them. Little Kate had to be taken in her carriage, and the two elder ones went with her. The rest of the day Meg and John amused themselves out of doors.

Molly then went to the kitchen and prepared dessert or pastry, made all arrangements possible at that hour for dinner, and attended to the lunch. She knew that in many a good boarding-house the luncheon, because there are only ladies to partake of it, is often a scrappy meal — odds and ends of cold meat, a few pickles, or beets and potatoes.

Instead of this kind of meal Molly knew it would not cost more than twenty-five cents extra to have something they might enjoy. If there was cold ham or corned beef in the house, then she would buy a couple of nice crisp lettuce, have hot biscuit made, and with some good cake she considered the luncheon a very appetizing one, with cocoa or chocolate for those who preferred it to tea. But when the meat was cold veal or mutton, or even roast beef, it was made into one of the appended savory dishes, and Molly reckoned the five cents' worth of stock used to heat them in was about all the extra expense. Sometimes on chilly days a nice clam or other soup preceded the lunch. While the party remained small, instead of having lunch on the large dining table, Molly had the leaves of the side table extended, a small table cloth spread, and the luncheon served on it; in fact, she did everything possible to avoid the conventional appearance of the boarding-house lunch, and trifling as such things may seem they made themselves felt. Generally the dish for luncheon could be watched while Molly attended to other things, made her wares for the Exchange or dessert for dinner.

After lunch Molly attended to her children, planned clothes, or saw friends till four, when down to the kitchen she went, saw that all was going on toward dinner, prepared anything that might be necessary, and when she had assured herself that if there was to be roast meat the oven was hot enough to brown it quickly so that there would be no gray or sodden joint at dinner time, and that Marta had all her instructions well in her mind, she would leave the kitchen for another hour, and then go down to remain until the dinner was cooked, so much depended on that hour. If she was there the vegetables would each be put on the fire at the proper time and boil in the right way. If she were absent, they might be over boiled and come too sodden to table. Scarcely even at a first-rate hotel are the vegetables properly prepared,

as Molly well knew, and she had resolved not
only would she buy choice ones (that is to say
she chose only such as were in their prime), but
she was determined that each should go on to
the table in the best condition; and it is quite
safe to say that some who ate them so did it for
the first time. Then the gravy and sauces she
gave her personal attention to.

One of her theories was that a good but inexpensive fish with a fine sauce was more appreciated than an expensive one with ordinary sauce;
therefore, fine cod with oyster sauce, or haddock
with Dutch sauce, were often part of the bill of
fare. But these sauces Molly hardly trusted to
Marta now that she had so many other dishes to
attend to, and when circumstances would prevent
her being on hand just before dinner to make
them she did so early, and left them to be heated
at the last in a hot water bath.

I have said already I can only indicate the
points on which Molly strove to improve on the
average boarding-house. I can only give such
details as will demonstrate that these points
were often not matters of expense, but only of
care; but when money did form an item it was
so small, compared with the result, that she preferred to make money more slowly, and to know
that her table was entirely satisfactory.

At the same time she made no impossible attempt. She would, for instance, have liked to have the pies always made of puff paste, or at least the rough puff; but this would not be possible if the family grew large, and she reserved that for patties or occasions. For ordinary use she made an excellent crust from the following recipe : —

PIE CRUST. Put one pound of flour in a bowl, mix with it a teaspoonful of baking powder, whip the whites of two eggs to a stiff foam, put them in the centre of the flour with a scant saltspoonful of salt, and make all into a stiff paste with about half a cupful of water. Flour the board, turn the paste on it, flour the rolling pin, roll it out to a thin sheet. Divide half a pound of butter into three parts. Take one, spread it in little bits over the paste, dredge a little flour over it, fold the paste in three, flour the rolling pin again, roll out as before, and spread the second part of the butter over it, dredge, fold, roll again, then add the third portion of butter, fold and roll again to the thickness for a pie, one third of an inch. This pastry has to be baked very quickly.

The cake, although generally some form of the "One, two, three, four" cake, yet by Molly's knowledge of the effect of five cents' worth of wine, or half that value of some uncommon blending of flavors, made the commonplace seem very far from it. Macaroons and other dainty cakes replaced the too frequent ginger snaps and cookies, and were less trouble. Because as she made them herself they cost barely thirty cents a pound.

Of course, soup was used almost daily. As a rule, it alternated with fish to precede the dinner; but sometimes Molly felt she could afford to have both, by using the less expensive kinds of soup, such as tomato cream soup, green pea soup (made from American canned peas), or cream of celery made from the coarser white branches of celery and the roots grated.

I give here a few recipes by which Molly gave economical variety to her table. If the reader will count up in her own mind how very few dishes (out of the hundreds that are in cook books) go to make up our daily fare, it will be seen that even half a dozen not usually used will add very much to a housekeeper's resources. One recipe which she had was a very favorite way of warming over cold meat.

Luncheon Dishes. Make a sauce with a large tablespoonful of chopped onion fried yellow in one ounce of butter. Stir into this a tablespoonful of flour, neither heaping full nor level, but slightly rounding. Let them cook together a few seconds, stirring all the time; pour to it a good half cup of boiling stock; stir till it boils, and one minute longer. Remove from the fire, and beat to it one egg ; the yolk alone will do if you have use for the white. Season with a scant half teaspoonful of salt, and the sixth of one of pepper. Butter a dish, cover each slice of meat thickly with the sauce, and lay it on the dish taking care they do not touch. When all are done set the dish on the ice. When cold dip each slice (which must be removed from the dish so as not to disturb the coating of sauce) in egg beaten with a tablespoonful of water, then in cracker crumbs, leaving a large quantity on a dish so that each slice can be smothered. When all the slices are crumbed, put a dripping pan on the stove with some nice beef dripping, let it get very hot, lay the meat in it, and put it a few minutes in a very hot oven just to brown the surface. These slices of meat may be dropped into deep boiling fat and fried brown. When done with, the cracker crumbs can be sifted and re-turned to the jar for future use ; *if not* sifted · they may spoil.

PIE OF COLD MEAT. This dish was only unusual as being better than the insipid one usually offered under that name. Slices of cold meat were laid in a dish, a little flour, salt, and pepper sprinkled over each layer until full, and then stock boiled down from a pint to half a pint poured over it, a crust put over, a hole cut in the centre, some little ornament to cover it, the whole brushed over with beaten egg, and baked one hour.

MEAT FRITTERS. Cold meat chopped fine, about an inch of boiled ham chopped with it (if liked), soften a tablespoonful of gelatine in a little stock or cold soup, melt a tablespoonful of butter in a small saucepan, add a tablespoonful of flour, stir them together over the fire till they bubble, make a scant cupful of stock hot, and stir the softened gelatine into it; when dissolved pour it to the butter and flour, stirring till it boils. When the sauce is smooth and thick, put to it the chopped meat (about a pint to this quantity), season with a small teaspoonful of salt and a quarter one of pepper, and from one to two teaspoonfuls of lemon juice. Taste before adding it, and when you find the flavor just changed, without being at all sour, put in no more. The seasoning must be rather high. When the mixture has all become hot together, without boiling after the meat is added, spread it out on a dish to get cold. It will then cut firm.

So far this recipe may seem troublesome, but it is little more so than properly made hash, where the onion has to be fried. The chopping is the same, and the sauce is not more trouble than frying the onion. If you have stock strong enough to jelly the gelatine is not required.

When the fritters are to be made make a

thick batter of a scant cupful of milk, one of
flour, two eggs, and a saltspoonful of salt, no baking powder. Make a dessertspoonful of the
meat mixture into balls, have a quantity of lard
smoking hot in a frying kettle, drop each ball
into a tablespoonful of batter, which turn carefully into the boiling fat. This quantity will
make a dozen and a half of fritters. While
Molly's family at lunch was so small she would
make half one day and leave the rest for croquettes another.

CROQUETTES are made exactly as above,
whether of cold meat or chicken, or lobster, so
far as the preparation goes; the difference is in
the final cooking. Make the meat mixture into
cork shapes (not *larger* than a cork), roll each
in beaten egg, then into cracker crumbs, taking
care every part is covered. These must be
dropped into fat so hot that they are yellow
brown in two minutes. Take them up and drain
on coarse paper, then serve.

Now croquettes made of cold meat are too
often merely hash balls, which crumble to pieces
under the fork; excellent things under their own
modest name, but unwelcome when they are
served as croquettes, which you expect to be
creamy when broken. Molly was able to prevent her boarders having this disappointment
with less than ten cents extra expense for each
day's luncheon. Sometimes she indulged them

still more, for if she happened to be making pies and there was a piece of dough as large as her own small fist left over, she would roll it out very thin, cut it into squares four inches by three, lay a bit of the fritter mixture on each, forming it into a finger or thin sausage, then would lap over one side the paste, moisten the upper surface, then fold the other side the paste to meet it and overlap half an inch. The ends were closed, and when they were brushed over with milk, if there was no remnant of egg, they were baked a pale brown.

Women will eat without grumbling very miserable lunches, provided the dinner is fair; but no one appreciates a dainty midday meal more than the woman with so little appetite that she cares very little if she eats or not, and does so more from habit than inclination. Very many women are like this.

Sometimes for variety Molly would have a can of lobster (which while much cheaper than fresh is excellent for cooking), and make lobster croquettes of one part and scalloped lobster of the other.

It will be observed that in the recipes given, and those that follow, stock is always used instead of water. This was one of the secrets of Molly's table, an open secret to all good cooks, but so little heeded by the general that it was never guessed. In the first place, it was a great economy. Of course, with soup several times a week there was no difficulty in having half a pint of stock always on hand, and in a family of half a dozen persons the bones of meat with *proper vegetables to flavor* would alone have sufficed ; but had this not been the case Molly would have considered it true economy to buy meat solely for the purpose. Twenty-five cents' worth of soup meat would make stock enough for gravies for a week.

Cold meat has parted with the greater part of its own gravy ; if warmed over with water it is tasteless unless very cleverly cooked. Warmed with good soup for gravy the meat is even better than fresh meat for many purposes. Therefore it was that those who did not like warmed-over meat till they lived with Mrs. Bishop did not guess they were eating it, so different was it from what they had known.

Let any skeptic who doubts try mince or hash or stew, and use not water, but good stock ; not broth of meat or bones and simple water, but well flavored with vegetables, such as would be good palatable soup if served at table, and then taking care that the meat never boils but steeps at boiling point in the ready thickened sauce ; and then consider if such dishes are not worth five cents (and a very little trouble) more than the tasteless ones she has been accustomed to associate with warmed-over meat.

CHAPTER XIX.

PROGRESS. — EXCHANGE GOSSIP.

ORDERS came in very plentifully now from the Woman's Exchange. Mrs. Tomes was greatly surprised. She had been very incredulous of any one succeeding, for a friend of her own had sent various articles to the Exchange, but they were returned stale on her hands. Another had seen her own articles neglected and others, not so good, put forward; and still another had gone there and been discouraged by being told nothing was needed; that she was welcome to leave what she liked, but they did not seem sanguine of success in selling her wares. All this Molly listened to; she had heard the same things before. She had known instances which seemed to corroborate them, and yet her own reception at the Exchange — and her experience — had been very pleasant! With regard to the first complaint (that articles were returned unsold) she felt that the managers might be less to blame than the consignor, for she had herself seen things there which she certainly would not have bought; and, most likely, such articles would go back to the makers, to their great surprise and discouragement. One lady connected with the direction had said : —

"We have a great struggle. Ladies subscribe on purpose to help their less fortunate friends, who bring to us articles that are unsalable because they are not perfect. But the consignor can't see that they are not just as good as can be bought. They want full prices for their wares, and, when they do not sell, they are sure there is favoritism."

"Then there is another trouble with women, — they *are* so unpunctual," this same directress had said. "A lady came to us in whom I was very much interested. She was evidently in great need, and anxious to turn her abilities to account. I asked what she could make, and among other things she mentioned *gumbo filé*, a dish which I was sure would find ready sale if properly made — if people only knew of it. To give it a fair chance, I told her to make a good deal. I invited half a dozen Southern friends to lunch with me at the Exchange on the day she appointed to send the dish. I knew that if they found they could buy their favorite *gumbo filé* ready prepared in New York there would be a large sale for it at once.

"Well, my friends came faithfully, but the

gumbo did not. It came the next day, however, at the promised hour, with regrets that for unforeseen reasons the consignor had been unable to send it the day before. Of course," said the speaker, " her chance had gone, and yet, I suppose, she might have been as successful as Mrs. X. had she been punctual and her *gumbo* good," — (mentioning a lady who makes an excellent living, and employs several assistants, only making rolls) — " and then, because I invited a few friends to give her specialty a start, it would be said by those for whom I had not done this that I had favored her."

Molly, therefore, had listened to Mrs. Tomes with respect, knowing that each person who related her experience had believed what she said, and that probably the truth lay between them all. One does not need to live many years in the world to learn how rare it is to find any one who can look on matters impartially. How rare are the women, or men, who can see that the cause of their own failure lies with themselves! Who can say to herself, " My work is not up to the mark, and therefore I don't succeed " ? — or, " I was not in time ; that 's why I lost the chance " ? And Molly could picture to herself the lady who sent the *gumbo* a day too late for the luncheon given for her benefit, believing that she had been ill-treated by having so much *gumbo* ordered and returned on her hands, and that the Exchange gave one no chance "unless you were a favorite."

Molly's own success, however, had not been due to favoritism, and she began to see that she would be obliged soon to choose between the boarding-house and the Exchange. The Mrs. X. of whom she had heard supported herself in comfort, and employed four assistants; in fact, was making as good an income as Molly would do with her boarders. But she rather feared to trust that her own success would be so complete as that; yet, very certainly, if her house became full, she could not do justice to both. Something of this sort she said to Mrs. Lennox.

"You are a lucky woman, Molly, to have a choice of two roads to success! But I was thinking it would be so, and I will now say to you something which I have been thinking of. If you do not like the idea, or have other plans, forget what I am going to propose. You know Jenny helps Mary in her green-house, indeed, one alone could hardly manage it; yet Jenny feels that she ought to do something for herself, and I thought that if she could help you with your cooking, she would be learning, and, as she has quite a taste that way, she might perfect herself in one or two things you make; therefore, if you do stop sending articles to the Exchange, she might continue."

Mrs. Lennox spoke with hesitation, but Molly quickly reassured her.

"Why, Mrs. Lennox! I am so glad that you suggested this, for I was wishing, if I could not do the two things properly without killing myself, that some one might benefit by the chance. Jenny never occurred to me, but she will be just the one."

Mrs. Lennox was very grateful to Molly, who assured her that the help Jenny would be just now to her — enabling her to earn the welcome money from the Exchange until her house should be full of boarders — made the obligation hers; for Jenny was so bright and so earnest that it took her a very short time to make "rough puff paste" just as Molly made it, and macaroons were learned in a couple of lessons. Now that she had such efficient assistance, Molly purposely enlarged the list of articles she sent away, and made pound cake and nun's cake, in order that Jenny might have a better chance later.

CHAPTER XX.

In the last chapter I have somewhat anticipated matters, for Molly had her house two
months before she began to see that the orders
from the Exchange were growing beyond her;
but, no doubt, the reader will like to learn how
she came out at the end of the first month finan-
cially. It will be remembered that she had
eighty dollars after paying for fuel, rent, milk,
and servants. She found that her housekeeping
expenses were as follows: —

Grocer, including flour and all sundries .	$20.00
Butter (20 pounds at 28 cents) . . .	5.60
Eggs (10 dozen at 25 cents)	2.50
Fruit and vegetables	10.00
Butcher, including fish	35.00
Sundry expenses	5.00
Gas	5.00
	$83.10

The wages of the laundress Molly did not

count, for the laundry was actually a business by itself, and Molly meant to reckon her profit and loss (she did not fear the last) on that account as separate. The boarders' washing almost paid the wages now, and did not take more than half the week. The laundress had nothing but the washing to do until it was finished, when, as agreed, she lent a hand in various ways. But with the house full of people, her time would be fully employed, and her board as well as wages would be more than paid, and the house laundry work would also be done without interrupting the cook. If she became as successful as she hoped, there might be too much work for one laundress, and then, of course, she would hire a woman to help by the day. She could not but feel that her future, by these figures, was very promising. She had fully expected to have to make up a larger sum, and was delighted at the smallness of the deficiency. She knew she had catered liberally, and that the two transient boarders who were coming the next month would cover the deficiency. She saw that with six boarders she would be able to pay all expenses, but she would make nothing but her own and her children's comfortable support (which is already making a great deal), she acknowledged. If she should be able to save ever so little outside of this, she would think herself a very fortunate woman. Of course, a month later, her coal bill would double, and before midwinter, it would cost four times what it did at present. The gas, too, would greatly increase; but two more boarders would go far to pay the difference.

But the time came, not many months later, when Molly had a dozen boarders, and then she did find herself with money to put away; and as she could always have had more boarders if she had been able to receive them, she had no losses from vacancies.

As soon as Jenny Lennox was able to make one article for the Exchange perfectly, Molly resigned the making of it and the proceeds to her. In this way, at the end of six months, Jenny had a business in her hands which would go on increasing so long as she kept her productions up to the required standard. Molly had gradually dropped it as she ceased to need the few extra dollars.

Jenny Lennox has not made a fortune through the Exchange, but she has and does make more than she could in any other way without leaving home, without capital, and without employing all her time. She clothes herself, and assists the narrow income of the family.

And now we can only glance at the next fifteen years of Molly's life, during which her children grew toward manhood and womanhood. Molly had prospered meanwhile by dint of faithful hard work. Not by any means easy had been those years of prosperity, but Molly had braced herself to encounter difficulties, and to endure annoyances. The battle of life she knew was not to be won by sitting in soft places. She encountered suspicion and injustice and discontent where she knew she ought only to have met with grateful confidence, and yet the sweet appreciation she also met with more than balanced it all. But the most exasperating hardship of her life was caused by the difficulty of finding faithful service.

Her difficulty began when she felt it due to herself to take a cook. She needed more time for marketing and housekeeping, as her boarders increased, and she began her quest. She wanted a competent person for plain cooking, and expected to pay good wages. Every housekeeper will know what befell Molly. The competent person with reference was engaged at twenty dollars a month, and a promise from Molly that if she found her valuable after six months to raise her to twenty-five, " because," she reasoned, " a really economical, good woman in the kitchen will be priceless to me, and the five dollars extra will be nothing, for she will save it."

Alas for Molly! She found the young woman actually knew no more of cooking than the average general servant. She could broil steak badly, roast meat the same, and make a vile pie. Because the cook was bad, Molly had no notion that her boarders must suffer, so she resumed her place in the kitchen. On the arrival of the cook she had given the children to Marta's care, who was devoted to them, and she could not recall Marta to her aid, for the new cook was not cleanly enough to change places with her. Therefore, for one month, Molly paid cook's wages to a woman who simply helped her in the kitchen, she herself doing the work. This seemed outrageous, but Molly learned that it was really not so very bad, compared with later experience, for the woman was good natured and respectful. She intimated, of course, that Molly's views were peculiar to herself, that everywhere else her cooking was thought good. The next experiment was far worse. Molly had sought far and wide, walked between aisles of hard-featured, unclean, disreputable looking women, all cooks, out of place, looking vainly for one of good face and respectable attire that she would be willing to introduce into her house. There did seem to be respectable waitresses, nurses, chamber maids, but no cooks.

At last, in despair, knowing she must have a

cook, she engaged the least truculent looking Hibernian she could find. She had a year's reference.

Molly went on the principle that unless you give a woman a chance to show what she can do, by leaving her uninterfered with for the first day or two, you can't tell what is in her. Therefore she gave her orders for breakfast as usual over night: hominy, graham muffins, broiled chops, fried potatoes. The potatoes were cold ones, which Molly usually had cut half an inch thick, floured, seasoned, and then fried, or rather *sauted* in fat till yellow brown one side, then turned and browned the other. They then made a handsome dish of fried potatoes. Molly paid her usual visit to the kitchen before seven, found the fire black, not yet burned up, and not likely to burn, being full of fresh coals.

"Why, Bridget, we shall never have breakfast on time, I 'm afraid," said Molly.

"Och an' don't you worry, ma'am; I was niver late wid a breakfast yet."

Bridget caught up an apron full of sticks as she spoke, and was proceeding to jab them down through the coals.

"No, Bridget, that will not help you at all. The mistake is in building the fire; you have not allowed the wood to burn sufficiently, for it is still black and smouldering underneath, and then

you put on all the coal at once. To-morrow if
you will make first a good wood fire by letting
it half burn through, then put on a few coals at
a time, you will find that by seven o'clock you
will have the kettle boiling and a hot oven."

While Molly spoke she took off the coals till
she came to the wood, which was already starting
up into fresh flames from the air let into it, then
she put on the lids, and said, "Now, Bridget, I
leave you to get breakfast. It will be too late
this morning for muffins; but if you put more
coal on when this has burnt bright, you will find
that the fire will be ready for broiling before
you need it."

Bridget had hitherto said nothing, but now
turned as Molly left the kitchen, and said, with
a laugh, "As if I naded any one to tache me to
make a fire! I that's cooked for the best av
families for twenty years."

Molly wisely refrained from noticing this
speech, but she concluded Bridget was not
likely to be an improvement on the last cook,
unless, indeed, her abilities should prove such as
to justify her in resenting interference.

When breakfast was served her doubts were
settled. The potatoes, instead of being fried as
she directed, had been chopped and fried in cool
grease; they were, consequently, grayish-white,
familiar enough to those who have been de-

pendent on the average boarding-house cook, but very distasteful to Molly. The chops blackened every plate on which they were put, and the hominy, which Molly was sure could not be sufficiently done, was really cooked to a paste. She could not understand how this had been managed until she began to eat, when she detected at once a slight taste of baking soda, and then she remembered hearing a woman say she was going to make a chicken pot-pie, after gossiping her morning away.

" But you've only three quarters of an hour. How can you make pot-pie. The chickens will need much longer ? "

"Oh, pshaw! Just slap a little carbonate of soda in with them, and they'll be tender." (Molly had partaken of the pot-pie at the given time; it was flat and bad as a pot-pie could be, but the chickens were almost *too* tender.) Undoubtedly her own cook had resorted to the soda-box to soften the hominy.

After this, Molly resolved to trust no more to her new cook. For a few days she managed, by convenient deafness, and by seeing to everything herself, to get along, Bridget constantly muttering "that she had cooked twenty years for millionaires, and it was strange she could n't do it for a lot of common boarders."

To be sure, the millionaires had not had such

"fusses and messes" as Molly wanted; they had "plenty of good meat." To all of which pleasant talk Molly paid no apparent heed. This woman had to be in the house a month, and for such mere expressions of opinion she could not be discharged. Therefore, unless Molly wanted to pay her a month's wages, and send her away at once, she must avoid provoking any open insolence.

Therefore, though she had to be daily in the kitchen, she got along for a' week, until one morning she arranged the fire for baking before going to market, and when she returned, ready to make patties, which required a very hot oven, she found all her arrangements changed, the cover off, and a small saucepan set down on the fire.

At this Molly's patience was nearly exhausted.

"Oh, dear! Bridget, the oven must be cold."

"Och, ye 've never enough fire in that stove to make it hot. Yer can't have hot ovens widout burning coals, that 's very sure."

It was this person's cue to treat Molly's instructions not to over-fill the fire-box with coal as "stinginess," her own idea being to fill up the stove until the coals reached the covers.

"But," said Molly, forcing herself to speak gently, "you don't understand the management of a range; if you take off the covers the heat " —

"Och, an' indade I understand the range as well as the man that made it, and better, may be."

In this sentence lay the key to at least one half the servant difficulty: the belief of the densely ignorant that they need no teaching.

Just here, perhaps, I may as well give one of the "messes" which I alluded to, a chapter or two back, as a dish which became famous among Molly's boarders, who little knew that it took the place — and cost little beyond the price — of the too prevalent hash.

MOCK TERRAPIN. A pint of nicely-flavored broth, vegetable soup, or stock, whichever is handy, and about two pounds of cold meat (lamb, veal, mutton, or beef), cut in small, inch squares, quite free from gristle or skin; two tablespoonfuls of butter, two of flour, and a small cup of fine cider or sherry. (The soup being already flavored will render other flavoring unnecessary.) Put the butter and flour into one saucepan over the fire; let the soup get boiling hot in another; stir the butter and flour till they bubble; pour the boiling soup to them, quickly stirring all the time. This should now look like smooth drawn-butter, slightly colored. Let it boil one minute; remove it from the fire to a spot where it will keep at boiling-point, but not boil. (On this depends the success of the dish, for, after the meat is in, it must steep *at boiling-point* half an hour, but not boil; a double boiler would make success certain.) Lay the meat in with a level teaspoonful of salt and a quarter one of pepper; stir all round; then add a small teacupful (or two wineglassfuls) of sherry or cider (cider will do instead of wine for any unsweetened dish), and leave it half an hour. Boil six or eight eggs quite hard (that is, for twelve minutes), lay them in cold water, to make the shells leave easily, remove the shells, cut each egg in thick slices, and, when the meat is done, pour the mock terrapin on a large platter, and cover with the sliced eggs. Round the edge of the dish, split pickled gherkins may be laid at intervals, and served with it; or cut lemon can be handed around.

This is a very large dish. For three or four persons one fourth the quantity can be made. This dish — wine, stock, and all — did not cost fifteen cents more than hash (that is, not one cent to each person). As Molly never had hash, without eggs to accompany it, the eggs used took the place of them; but the dish is excellent without.

The words used by Bridget in the foregoing conversation were less insolent than others Molly had forced herself to ignore, but they, and the vexation of finding her work delayed, were the last straws. She resolved to sacrifice the rest of the month's money rather than endure the woman in the kitchen another hour, and within the hour she left with twenty unearned dollars in her pocket, and left the whole household with light hearts that they were free of her. The work without her vulgar presence seemed almost like play.

From this time Molly gave up engaging so-called "cooks." She found it better to take a newly-landed girl, although she might have to spend a couple of months in the kitchen with a likely one. The unlikely she discharged as soon as she discovered the uselessness of trying to train her. The daily supervision after, of course, practically made of Molly a sort of head cook the greater part of the time (for, in fifteen years, she had trained and lost several cooks); yet, on the whole, she found her plan the best, for at least she did not, for the first year, pay large wages, and it was not such hard work to struggle with the ignorance that knows itself, as to struggle with the impudent ignorance that believes itself knowledge.

Therefore I say, although they were cheerful, prosperous years for Molly, they were years of hard work.

But of late, even this matter of engaging a green girl was not an easy one. Castle Garden is no longer what it was, for others have found out the better value of the confessedly incompetent, and for every girl there are a dozen places waiting.

The proper education of her children had been a matter of the gravest thought and care. Molly's idea of education was that it was better for children to learn a few things well than many imperfectly. She rather clung to the old-fashioned notion that reading, writing, and arithmetic should be mastered before other branches were gone into. Reading seemed the gateway to all knowledge, and if a child showed a decided taste for any particular branch of study every effort should be made to help it to pursue that branch. It did not seem to her — and she studied the matter from its results on girls who had gone through the usual high-school course — that the little bit they learned of astronomy, physiology, geology, and half a dozen other sciences, for the useful study of which a lifetime is hardly too much, added anything to their usefulness as women, or to their pleasures. Not that the *thorough* study of any one of these things would not have been a great accomplishment, and she would have encouraged to the utmost any inclinations to a special study of any *ism* or *logy* her girls might have shown. Her theory was that well-directed reading, that is to say, historical reading, in which the references were looked up; travels, in which the same plan was pursued, would give as much general information as is required to make an intelligent, well-informed woman.

Molly was not prepared to do battle for her opinions on this subject, nor was she very sure that she was right; but she did think over the matter very earnestly. She paid special attention for a year or two to every "girl graduate " she saw, and in the end she adopted for Meg the old system of learning the three R's, and watched for any special talent or taste she might have. Music, from the first, it was evident she would do nothing with, although she was anxious to learn ; but she had no ear, — could not catch the tune even of the childish nursery jingles. But Molly did believe most thoroughly in Doctor Johnson's dictum, that as many languages as you know, so many lives you live, and knowing how much her own familiar knowledge of French, and less knowledge of German, had added to her pleasure in life, she was determined that her children should benefit by it.

For this reason, as soon as a living was assured, Molly cast about for a French nurse. It was easy enough to find one, but the one she

wanted was not of this kind. She wanted a
simple, country girl, even if she knew nothing
at all of civilized life as we understand it. Of
course, she did not want a mere goatherd, who
could not read or write; but a French Marta
would have suited better than a nimble-minded,
and still more nimble-fingered, Parisian. After
some months of effort, a Swiss girl was found
who spoke fairly good French, and no English
at all, and within a year from the time she came
Meg, John, and Kate were chattering to her
glibly.

Many people wondered at a sensible woman
like Molly caring to have her children learn
French from an uneducated girl. Her answer
was this : —

" If I could afford to have a French lady with
me all the time I would not think of this; but
that is out of the question, and fluent conversa-
tional French is more valuable, even if the accent is not so good, than school French which,
as a rule, only serves, after years of study, to
enable the student to stumble through a page of
reading, and to write, with infinite difficulty, a
French letter; and even this will drop from
one in a few years. Now I reason this way:
we all speak broken French, even when most
fluent. There will be the English accent.
Well, a little more or less of accent will not

be of much importance, — but then I really do not see that it need necessarily be so. Many people, not rich enough to pay fancy wages to fancy nurses, have a young Irishwoman to take care of their children. And, more often than not, she will have the richest brogue, but our children are not affected thereby; they have no brogue. It is true, Meg has told me once or twice that Marta was 'just after doing so and so,' and a few other locutions of the sort, which she will drop in a very short time."

" Yes, because you will correct her."

" Well, I shall correct her French, so far as I am able; but what I think is, that when she comes to use books she will correct herself as naturally as she will correct her Hibernian English; and even if she does not, any fluent, conversible French short of patois — and, of course, I shall not take a girl who uses that — will be better than the usual useless school knowledge; and I shall watch for opportunities of doing better for them. I may meet with a French lady who, in exchange for board, will talk to the children a stated time in the day."

And thus it was that as Meg, John, and Kate became ready for school, they already were familiar with oral French and German, for Molly had never lost her habit of speaking German to Marta.

I said the worst hardship of Molly's life was the difficulty of finding suitable assistance in return for a good home and liberal wages; but there was another element of vexation that had helped to cloud her path, and that was her husband's family. Of course, their plan, so triumphantly unfolded to Molly, had failed, as she knew it must fail, and they were much worse off for the experiment.

Then had come other equally wild schemes, all based on the necessity of living in the same apparent style that they were brought up in, the most disastrous being an arrangement with a very elegant French baroness to take the house and board the family for part of the rent. The house was quickly filled with elegant foreigners, and all went joyously for six months. Madame did not pay the rent, but had magnificent diamonds and excellent reasons, which she gave as security.

At the six months' end, however, Mrs. Bishop, Senior, was summoned by telegraph to Greenfield; Molly was dangerously ill. The daughters were away, having taken their father to Clifton Springs.

Mrs. Bishop started on her journey, and, on reaching Molly's house, found her quite well; no such telegram had been sent. Molly had never believed in the " Baroness," and, when she heard the story, instantly started back with Mrs. Bishop, and found, as she expected, that the "Baroness" had departed with her friends.

It is needless to say the diamonds were splendid paste; and, worse than all, Mrs. Bishop found that her own tradesmen had supposed they were supplying her, and everything had been charged to her that had been ordered to the house.

In all these crises Molly's common sense was called on to straighten out matters; but so long as there was any choice whatever, her services only were accepted, — never her advice. Then came a time when, having wasted everything, they had to sell the house, and go to live in a very small way in Belgium, on the proceeds. Had they rented it as soon as they lost their money, they would have received a comfortable income from it. But their transference, which was the doom of their gentility, was a blessing to Molly.

CHAPTER XXI.

MOLLY'S PLANS FOR MEG. — DR. MILNE SPEAKS.

MOLLY had very carefully watched her children for indications of any special talents they might show. Meg, as the elder, she had expected would develop her tastes and inclinations before the others ; but she watched for her dawning talent in vain. She was generally bright and capable, but her forte seemed to be in helping her mother. When she was fourteen, between lesson hours she took entire charge of the dining table. (Molly's boarding-house, perhaps I should have stated, had assumed large and handsome proportions, and was widely known. She had been able to buy the house and build on to it.) She arranged the fruit and flowers for breakfast with rare taste, and introduced all sorts of pretty fancies. The napkins were always changed regularly, and the table-cloth was spotless and without creases, under Meg's superintendence. This one duty, which she could trust with utmost confidence to her, was a great relief to Molly, small as it was.

Then the little girl's delight was to assist in kitchen work ; she could make meringue, whip cream solid, and arrange salad as well as any grown woman. Molly was delighted to see these womanly tastes develop, and yet as years went on and Meg only grew more expert as a cook, and showed no taste for the arts by which her mother had hoped she would be able to make a living, she was disappointed. Of course, she confided her trouble to Mrs. Welles, who made light of it.

"I don't think you need worry, Molly, about Meg's livelihood ; so pretty a girl will be married before you can look round. I think I've seen more than one young man at church pay more attention to Meg than to his prayer-book."

"Oh, but it is against all my ideas and principles to bring a girl up only to marry. Knowing something by which she may earn a living will not prevent that, and if anything happens to me I want her to be independent."

"To tell the truth, my dear, while I think something is quite as likely to happen to Meg herself as to you, if anything *did*, Meg could carry on your business just as well as you, and make a home for her brother and sister." [1]

---

[1] This is no exaggeration. I know of one young girl under twenty, who had been brought up to help her mother who had had for years a large and fashionable boarding-house on Fifth

" I believe she would be quite able," laughed Molly; " but as I don't mean to die, if I can help it, until Kate is grown up, I prefer Meg to know how to make a living independent of me. And neither she nor I can decide what she is most fitted for."

" What do you think of letting her go through the cooking school ? We may teach her everything between us, but we could not so well teach her to teach, as she would be taught in going through the regular drill.".

" I have thought of it, and Meg takes to the idea. I don't know any field of woman's work where there is so much room."

" Well, then, if you desire, let her learn all she can in the New York schools, then trust her to Cuthbert and me, and when we go to London next year we will let her go through South Kensington. She will then be able, should she not marry, to open a training school of her own."

Molly gladly assented to the plan, and on consulting Meg found her quite willing, her only objection being to leaving her mother for so long a time while she studied ; but Molly succeeded in comforting her on this head, and that fall Meg began to go to the city for lessons.

Avenue, New York. On the sudden death of the mother, the young girl stepped into her place and, young as she is, I hear the house still goes on its prosperous way.

As the time came for Meg to leave with Mrs.
Welles for Europe, Molly's courage almost gave
way. How could she spare her? Only now
did she realize how dear and helpful her elder
daughter was; how little thought she had ever
had for herself, and how she had clung to her
mother, seeming instinctively to know when she
was sad, even at the earliest age, and would
slide her little hand in Molly's, without a word.
All these endearing little ways she had retained,
and very few mothers and daughters were so
much to each other as Molly and Meg.

And yet there came a reason which reconciled
Molly to the parting. For some time there had
been two or three young men trying to be attentive to Meg, which Molly had quietly observed
and ignored; but as time went on, another, who
seemed bolder and more persevering, appeared
on the scene, and as his attentions became more
marked, Molly thought it an excellent thing
that her daughter was going away. George
Milne, the young man who seemed bent on becoming her son-in-law, was one that even an am-
bitious mother might have approved. He was a
physician who had come to Greenfield to assist
Doctor Price, and within a year the old doctor
and Molly's dear friend died.

Doctor Milne had been so successful that he
found himself at eight-and-twenty with a fine

practice and a growing reputation outside of Greenfield, for he had written some excellent papers on the treatment of the ear, which had been well spoken of in medical circles.

But in spite of this, Molly felt that Meg ought to see more of the world before her affections were engaged. She fancied she had seen that Meg treated Doctor Milne differently from others who fluttered round her. She was less frankly unreserved with him, and once or twice when Molly had mentioned his name, watching her daughter as she did so, she saw the sweet color rise in her cheek, and that she made an excuse to speak of something else. These Molly knew were signs of interest that Meg displayed for no other. But as yet her mother thought it was but a passing fancy, that her journey to Europe would cure. Molly forgot how prone an innocent girl is to hero-worship; how easy it is to make a hero of a good-looking young man, whose praises she hears on all hands; of whose disinterested kindness to the sick poor she is well aware. No wonder sweet Margaret Bishop felt her heart flutter when Doctor Milne seemed to single her out for attention. It seemed almost like a dream to her, and she feared her vanity was leading her astray when she fancied his dark eyes sought hers far more frequently than was necessary.

But all such innocent doubts were suddenly ended one morning as she was coming from market, just a week before she was to sail for Liverpool. She had an errand which took her some little distance out of the town, and as she was returning homeward, a doctor's buggy passed her. A hundred yards ahead it stopped, Doctor Milne sprang out on the grassy roadside, and the buggy was driven slowly on.

For a moment Meg looked with a vague curiosity, wondering why the doctor stopped where there was no house. It was not till he was approaching her with rapid steps, and she saw the greeting smile, that she realized he had seen her and had stopped on purpose to speak to her. It did not even then dawn on her that he had any motive in seeking her. It was certainly very pleasant to be singled out for such special attention from her hero; beyond this she did not think.

"Miss Bishop, I heard only last night that you are going away," he said, rather eagerly, "and — and there is something I have to say to you. You must excuse my being so abrupt, but I could not let you go without speaking."

He had turned and was walking by her side. Meg was silent; her heart fluttered wildly, she hardly knew why, and she did not know what to think. It could not be possible that — oh, it

could not be possible! such an insignificant girl
as herself!

But it was. The next moment he had recov-
ered from his momentary embarrassment, and
was telling her with rapid, eager words how he
loved her and wanted her for his wife; how he
had meant to wait and let her know him better,
but when he heard of this intended trip he did
not dare to wait. Now might he go with her
and speak to her mother?

What Meg said she did not know herself, so
of course I cannot tell. She was filled with joyful pride, and she really did not know whether
the feeling she had for Doctor Milne was anything but this or not.

The doctor was not nearly so inexperienced as
she was, and was not too much discouraged by
her manner. He saw the dewy light in her eyes
and the heightened pink flush, and knew that he
was not distasteful to her; she was merely
overcome by the unexpected.

"You don't dislike me, at least?" he asked,
not in the smallest doubt as to the answer.

"Oh, no, no," —and the warmth of the denial
spoke volumes.

"Then I am satisfied. I will not see Mrs.
Bishop now, but may I come to-night?"

Meg drew a breath of relief; that was just
what she wanted — a quiet hour with her
mother, and time to think of things.

"Then I will leave you now." He pressed her hand and left her.

Somehow Meg, who had not dreamed of being lonely before, now felt suddenly alone, as if something warm and pleasant had fallen from her.

CHAPTER XXII.

MOLLY'S DECISION.

MEG slipped into the house when she reached home and went to her room. She did not want to see even her mother until she had had time to think, and, above all, to wonder — after all, a great wonder! How it could be possible that *he* loved her and wanted her to be his wife was her predominant thought, and, amid it all, she tried to find out what was her feeling towards him. While she was still trying to make out that it was impossible she could love a man of whom she knew so little, although she *liked* him — ah! more than she could express — her mother entered.

" Why, Meg, are you sick? I saw your hat down stairs, and that told me you were in. What is the matter, my darling?" asked Molly, anxiously; for a glance at Meg's flushed, but very happy face, reassured her as to her health.

Meg threw her arms round her mother.

"Oh, mother! I — I met Doctor Milne."

"Oh!" Molly's "Oh" was one of sudden

enlightenment. " Then, I dare say, I can guess what he talked about; but tell me, all the same."

Molly's arm was around Meg to assure her of a sympathizing listener, and then the story was told.

" Well, darling, and so he is coming to see me to-night? "

" I think so, mother dear."

" I suppose, Meg, you don't care for me to say ' yes ' to him? " asked Molly, with a steady mouth, but a smile in her eyes.

Meg started. It had not occurred to her that her mother might wish her to refuse him. The very moment that idea came to her, she was very sure she could not do it.

" I don't know. I like him better than any one I ever saw; and, oh! he is so good."

Molly laughed.

" I 'll tell you what I have to say about this, Meg. Doctor Milne is very nice and very suitable; but you know nothing of his disposition, nor he of yours. I could not let you engage yourself to him. You have seen too few men; but if — when you return from Europe and have carried out our plans, just as if there was no Doctor Milne — he still wants you and you care for him, then I shall be very glad to say, ' Bless you, my children ! ' "

Meg was silent, and Molly said : —

" What do you think, dear ? "

Meg gave a little sigh.

" Whatever you say *is* best *will* be best, mother."

But when Doctor Milne came that night and heard Molly's decision, he was by no means so docile. It was very hard, he said, to wait a year in uncertainty; but even when (being more reasonable and thoughtful than most men of his age) Molly had brought him to see that it was best, both for himself and Meg, that she should see more of the world and know her own mind, he yet could not agree to the necessity of her proposed course of study.

" Dear Mrs. Bishop, surely such a course is not necessary. Margaret lets me hope she will be my wife. I shall *not* change, and it is my dearest hope that absence will not lessen her liking for me. Why, then, need she prepare for a single life ? "

Molly laughed.

" She is by no means doing so. Mrs. Welles prepared for and began a successful career, which did not prevent her marriage, and she is, in every way, a gainer by the experience. Then I must remind you that Meg will not be *engaged* to you. You must not even attach too much importance to her liking for you — she has seen so few men — and she must go away without the shadow of a tie."

"I think that is hard, Mrs. Bishop. I assure you, if Meg engages herself conditionally to me, I will make no reproaches should she find some one on her travels that she prefers; or if she does not, and yet cannot marry me, I shall acquiesce in what she thinks best for her happiness. If you consent to this, it will give me some feeling of happiness, and will not tie her."

But Molly was firm. She knew Meg too well not to be sure that even a conditional engagement would tie her conscience and cause her acute suffering should she find she had mistaken her feelings, and she was also firm in her resolve that Meg should go through her appointed studies in spite of Doctor Milne's protest.

"If my daughter becomes your wife, and, later, anything happens to reduce your means or you die, she will not find herself like so many women, with no one thing they can do thoroughly well. It is my belief, if any woman knows one art thoroughly well, she will never lack the means of living, even if her art be only that of knitting or crocheting."

"But my wife will be well provided for, even should I die within a year of our marriage."

"Well and good; but she, or any woman, will be the better for what she will know."

When Molly spoke in this tone, any one with the smallest discrimination knew that further argument was useless.

Mrs. Welles, who, of course, had been told of Meg's new prospects, agreed with her mother in thinking no change should be made in their plans.

"Of course, we will do as we said; but you may be quite sure Meg will be Mrs. Milne."

"What makes you think so? I have observed her closely, and really think she has no deep affection; that her pleasure in his offer is a mixture of hero-worship and romance."

"Mothers do not sometimes see so far as others; but of one thing I am sure: a man like Doctor Milne does not come into the life of a girl like Meg and go out very readily. I don't believe the flock of *jeunesse doré*, with whom I intend to surround her in Europe, will do anything but deepen her present feelings."

"Well, well; so be it! I, for one, shall rejoice that it should be so. Then I should stand a chance of having my dear girl always near me."

If Molly could have looked into her daughter's shy heart as she returned Milne's entreating look, when he begged her to try not to forget him, by one of reassurance, she would not have doubted the result more than Mrs. Welles did.

About John's bent, Molly was not long in doubt. It had been a keen desire with her that her son's taste and talents should incline him to the profession of a civil engineer. She watched him from babyhood, and hoped to see him display some preference for mechanics. She read articles herself (and talked afterward to him) on the wonders of engineering science; but she could never arouse the least enthusiasm in him. He listened restlessly, and eagerly waited for something more interesting. Molly sighed to think her dear wish would be thwarted.

"Why are you so anxious for John to be an engineer?" asked Mrs. Welles.

"Long before I ever knew I should have a son, I thought it was the noblest profession a man could have. Even now I thrill with enthusiasm when I read of its great achievements. It seems to me, too, to open a career that depends on talents and work done, with which chance or luck has less to do than with most others. Then I have always observed, too, wherever one meets a civil engineer, he is never out of employment. I remember once meeting two young Irish gentlemen, who had just arrived in Canada at a time when everything was stagnant. We made their acquaintance at the hotel, and my husband and I pitied them, fearing their high hopes and small funds would soon be exhausted, and that they would go to swell the crowd of poor young fellows out of employment; but instead of that, before the week was out, both had employment. They found there was no opening for engineers till spring. Accordingly one went to a patent lawyer, and was immediately employed as a draughtsman; the other got surveying to do. Both were fairly well paid. When I congratulated them on their good fortune, one of them laughed joyously, and said : —

"'Oh, you never need fear for an engineer who knows his work in all its branches, and is steady! He will tumble on his feet wherever he is.'

"Mr. Bishop recalled several instances that bore out the statement, and I have noticed it since. For all these reasons I have so earnestly hoped that John would become an engineer that, I fear, I shall be terribly disappointed should he not."

"Perhaps if he begins to study for it the liking may come."

"Yes; if he shows no special disposition for anything else, and seems to have any talent for mathematics, I will advise him to choose that profession; but if he has leanings in another direction, I will not venture to cross his tastes. That is too dangerous an experiment."

"Not even if he wished to be a musician or an actor?"

Molly hesitated. She had no prejudice against either profession; indeed, a fine musician or great actor may well be proud of his art. But the lower walks are so low, so full of pitfalls, and offer so little future to manhood, that Molly felt, without knowing just how to say it, that nothing less than the drawing of undoubted genius ought to justify the choice of either. John was fourteen when this conversation took place, and Molly was quite sure he had neither dramatic nor musical genius.

"If he wished to be either, without showing talent of the most marked kind, I should oppose those professions with all my might and authority; but, as he has displayed no such talent yet, we need not consider them. But if he shows a strong desire for any calling to which he is fitted, I shall forward his views, however averse I may be; for I don't want a young man of twenty to come to me and say : —

"'Mother, I have obeyed you, and wasted my time. I can never be anything but what I wanted!'"

About this time a professor of chemistry was engaged at the school John attended to lecture and illustrate by experiment the science of chemistry. This was the first thing in which John seemed to become deeply interested. From that time Molly lived in dread of being blown up.

More than once miniature explosions had led to
her forbidding further experiments, which would
be rescinded when he told her he was going to
do something as safe as blowing soap bubbles,
and read the innocent directions from a book on
elementary chemistry; and then would follow
days with hands stained by acids and gaseous
odors filling the basement, to a spare room of
which, he and his hobby had been relegated.
At last Molly compromised the matter by telling
him that if he did not dabble with chemicals until he really understood them she would get him
special instruction; and when assured that he was
in no danger of blowing himself up she would
fit him up a small laboratory, provided his ardor
had not meanwhile evaporated.

Molly had known so many boys with hobbies
which were ridden ardently for a few months
and then dropped into the limbo of forgotten
things, that she fully expected John's craze to
be as transient; yet, as the knowledge would always be valuable, she made arrangements for
him to have extra lessons, just as she would have
bought him a bicycle as a thing innocent in itself, useful for development, and a pleasure to
him, little dreaming that in the boy's hobby
might lie his life-work.

She who had watched keenly for signs and
portents did not recognize this for a sign when

she saw it, because she had not been thinking of chemistry as a possible profession; and yet when his instructor later on told her that her son was an enthusiast in the science, and would certainly make an admirable chemist, she could but ask herself, why not? There was certainly no reason, except that she had never happened to know of a boy being brought up to be a scientific chemist.

She consulted Mr. Welles, who gave it as his opinion that if the boy really loved the science there could be no more promising career open to him. "It is not overcrowded by brainy men, and brains and enthusiasm will as surely tell in it as in your pet engineering."

And so John became a student of chemistry, and in deciding his own career he unconsciously influenced that of Kate.

CHAPTER XXIII.

MRS. WELLES'S PLANS. — MEG'S DIARY.

MOLLY had begged Mrs. Welles not to add in any way to the allowance she had considered sufficient for Meg. She had somewhat regretted that her daughter was going in company with a woman of large means; she would have liked her to know something of the thrifty life a student usually has to live, because she knew in this way only could Meg acquire an intimate knowledge of London life and ways. Living in expensive lodgings Meg would never do this; but of course the mother could not quarrel with the opportunity her daughter had had, and therefore when accepting Mrs. Welles's offer Molly only said, "She is going under too luxurious auspices; I wish she could live something of the life that you and I did, part of the time at least."

Mrs. Welles laughed and said, "I don't suppose Meg will quarrel with her chances of enjoying some of the luxuries of London life."

Nothing more was said; but when Meg and Mrs. Welles had paid their tribute to the sea

(for both suffered seasickness), and could begin
to believe that life was worth living, Mrs. Welles
told Meg of a project she had, leaving her to decide on it. Happily Mrs. Welles, strong-willed,
clear-minded woman as she was, had not the
manner of treating young people as if they could
not have a will or taste, but must submit themselves entirely to their elders, — a manner that
is always exasperating to the youthful mind.

"Meg, I have been thinking of a little plan,
and Cuthbert is quite willing we should carry it
out; but as you have come with me for a year's
enjoyment as well as study, I will do nothing to
disappoint you. If you object to roughing it,
say so, and the plan shall drop. Mr. Welles, as
you know, has to go to Russia to see to affairs
there, and may be away some months. My plan
is to put Lois for study with my old friend
Madame Ferani, who is a thorough artist and an
excellent woman, and who will tell me, quite re-
gardless of whether she will thereby gain or lose
a pupil, whether Lois has the remarkable talent
she seems to have, or not. If, after a trial,
Madame Ferani thinks it worth while to give
her more than the usual advantages, I shall enter her as a pupil in Madame Ferani's studio,
and arrange my own course according to it. I
had some thought of taking a furnished house
midway between the studio and the South Ken-

sington Museum, so as to suit you both. We could then lead a homelike life, see friends, etc.

"Now it is only the latter part of the programme that I thought I would alter. Your mother wished you might live just the old life she and I lived. I said nothing, but her words roused old memories, and the idea grew upon me. I, too, would like to renew my youth in that way. There was no privation, but, of course, no luxuries whatever. We used to plan and economize for every pleasure we enjoyed, and yet what happy days they were! I don't care to go back to the economy unless I can do it just in the old neighborhood; but I must say I would like to see if Cambridge sausages and pigeon pies will taste as good now, eaten, not as part of a meal, but as the meal itself, as they did when they were rather rare luxuries, being more expensive than most kinds of food."

Meg enjoyed the idea. She had heard her mother talk of old days and the way they lived in London; the many little economical pleasures they had, until that part of her mother's life seemed as familiar as her own; and she had almost regretted that Mrs. Welles's means made it natural to lead the conventional life of well-to-do people.

"Then that is settled. We will go to the Alexandre Hotel. Dear me, don't I remember its being built, and thinking what a very luxurious place it was. Luxurious hotels were not so general when I was a girl as now. Comfort and dinginess sufficed then. And when Cuthbert and I stayed there the last time we were in London, how he did abuse it! and certainly it did not seem anything very splendid by the side of the more modern houses. But it will never lose its charming situation. The front windows look into Hyde Park, Rotten Row, and the Drive. That alone is worth a great deal ; but when you sally forth, turn to your right, and in three minutes you are at Hyde Park corner, in five at Piccadilly. Turn to your left, and ten minutes' walk (if you can resist looking about you) will take you to South Kensington Museum.

" But, delightful as the situation is, I should not care to make a home there for more than a few days ; so I propose we stay there for a week, and from there look out for lodgings in some of the smaller streets in Kensington or Brompton, where we can be as Bohemian as we like. Shall we do that ? "

" I shall be delighted."

And the more Meg thought of the matter, the more delighted she was, and made a resolution to keep a diary for her mother and mail it once a week. This she began on board the steamer, and continued faithfully all through her stay in

London. It was very bright reading for any one, and who will not understand the pleasure it was (not unmixed with tears, however) for Molly to read of Meg's wanderings in the neighborhood she had known so well; how Mrs. Welles pointed out their favorite bun shop, the pastry cook's where they had bought their dainties, the small circulating library to which they had subscribed, and told her how few of these had changed hands in all the years that had passed. She even described how the young woman in the pastry cook's who used to be called the "Knightsbridge beauty" had become a still coquettish spinster, who wore her hair in exactly the same way as when Molly had admired her, only that the tendril-like locks that had made her youthful brow so charming made the faded, sunken temples look still older. All the pretty little ways she had had, Mrs. Welles said she had still, only somehow they did not look so pretty at forty as at twenty or so.

All this and very much more Molly read in that dear diary, with tears and smiles. But this part of their experiences followed some time after her settlement in London, although quite as amusing was the account of their life on shipboard and their landing.

"You remember, dear mother," wrote Meg from Liverpool, "dear Aunt Charlotte's sensi-

tiveness about the English climate, how she protested against Mr. Welles's abuse of it. Well,
she has given in at last, and declares she will
never defend it again, it did serve her such a
bad trick. The day before we landed was so
lovely! There was a party of young girls on
board, enthusiastic about everything, and as
every bit of land with a well-known name came
in view, they had a bit to quote or a novel to
refer to in which it was mentioned, and Mrs.
Welles was delighted with them. We came in
sight of the Skelligs about ten o'clock at night,
but as there was a lovely moon they were visible,
and these girls were in raptures.

"'Oh, there are the Skelligs! we are really
"Off the Skelligs"!' Then followed a discus-
sion about Jean Ingelow's most delightful book.
And the next day Snowdon and the Great Orme's
Head were greeted with equally delighted recog-
nition.

"'And isn't the weather perfect! Why, I
did not know they ever had such weather as this
in England!'

"Mrs. Welles looked on with glistening eyes
of triumph, and said: ' No, I suppose Americans
believe the sun never shines, and we never see
a blue sky until we leave our own country. I
wonder they never ask themselves how it is that
roses and many other flowers never attain such

perfection anywhere else; and let me tell you if
you are in London in spring you will find rhodo-
dendrons and other American plants in such
glorious beauty as you never saw out of doors
in their native land.'

"I, too, gloried a little in the fact that Old
England, which is dear to me because you love
it so, was showing herself so beautiful to us.
As we approached Liverpool, Mr. Welles in-
formed us that there was every chance of our
landing in the afternoon; the captain was making every effort. We had hardly hoped for it,
but as the news grew more certain that we
should be in time to cross the bar, we all has-
tened to our staterooms and got our things together. The stewardess stripped the beds, and
there was all the commotion of leaving the vessel, when, lo! in a minute everything changed.
We had been so busy below that we had not
noticed a growing darkness; when we reached
the saloon we found it crowded with people all
cloaked and ready for shore, with their hand
baggage around them; but, instead of the usual
good-tempered chatter going on, all were in a
state of consternation.

"Mr. Welles went to see what the trouble
was, and came to tell us that a fog had fallen.
I did not realize what that meant to us, and I
laughed; for I really was anxious to see a real
English fog, of which I had heard so much.

" ' I 'm much afraid we shall have to remain on board all night, after all.'

" ' What ! ' I said. 'And we are all ready, and the vessel is in such good time ! '

" ' Yes; but the captain thinks the tender will not be able to find us in the fog.'

" And so it turned out; and such a forlorn-looking crowd as we were, with our light baggage all about us, until ten at night, when word came that we positively could not land ! Dear Aunt Charlotte was *so* vexed, although she bore Mr. Welles's jokes very well. And such confusion as there was !—such objurgation of stewards and stewardesses !—for we had seen all our sheets in a mixed heap in the morning; yet the beds were remade, and they pretended that they had been able to fish out the sheets that belonged to each bed ; needless to say we slept in our rugs that night. Next morning, when the fog had partially cleared and we were told the tender was alongside, and had gone on deck, Aunt Charlotte told me she never would again say a word in defense of the climate, for although it had ' cleared,' we could not see people at the other end of the deck, and, when I looked up, I saw in the sky something round and whitish that reminded me very much of the way the lumps of ice looked in tumblers of water at the hotel table in Cincinnati. Don't you remember? I could hardly believe it was the sun ! "

And so on, for months, came this diary, and it was full of London experiences; sometimes giving a full account of a cooking lesson, and, at others, little details of their own lives, — how they managed to have little dinners and suppers at a small expense; how an art student, with whom she had made acquaintance, managed to live on two dollars and a half a week; the little delicacies she cooked in her own room, living ever so much better than many who boarded cheaply, but yet paid double what she spent. In all this, Meg's share of her mother's practicability was shown in the fact that she gave recipes and expenses always as part of the subject.

Monday evenings Doctor Milne spent with Molly. It was the day Meg's letters usually arrived, and at first she read him parts of them; then, as she really grew fond of him, she read the whole. Mrs. Lennox and her family often joined them, and, as the diary became more interesting, they all came regularly. But as Molly read these effusions of her daughter, she began to suspect a fact, which was confirmed by Mr. Lennox's saying: —

"Your daughter need not have gone so far to find an avocation; her evident vocation is resident. The girl of her age who can write so graphically as that is going to do something with her pen!"

Doctor Milne's eyes kindled, and he said quietly : —

" That is what I think. This is too valuable and too good not to be published."

And this was Molly's opinion, too ; and, therefore, we will dip no more into the diary, which Doctor Milne, with Molly's delighted consent, began at once transcribing on the heavier paper that would find favor with a publisher, writing, as all aspirants for print must do, " on one side the paper only," so that when Meg should return, she would find she had written a book without knowing it.

CHAPTER XXIV.

KATE'S VOCATION.

KATE had been the one delicate member of the Bishop family. But for her, no doctor's services would have been needed, and year by year Molly had dreaded that each would be the last of her darling; but after her seventh year, although they had all grown to think of her as an invalid, and to look on her fragile appearance as a sign of weakness, as a matter of fact she grew strong, and had as few ailments as others.

Nevertheless, she had been so tender a flower that Molly could hardly believe she was to have her for long, and never found courage to make plans for her future. Thus she was allowed to study in a desultory fashion, not altogether unsatisfactory as to results.

But if her mother did not dare to look forward for her, she did so for herself, and from the age of five, when she announced that when she grew up she meant to keep a candy store, because she would then *always have change*, to the time when she said that she would be a dressmaker, was always planning for being "grown up." This last decision lasted so long, and the child showed such skill in making doll's clothes, that it really did seem as if her own judgment was right, especially when, as she grew into a tall, slim girl of fourteen, she arranged her own frocks with a cleverness that insured them a peculiar grace. She was very fond, too, of arranging the drapery of Meg's and her mother's dresses. Sometimes she would do wonders with a shawl; and as Meg grew to be her mother's right hand in both kitchen and dining-room, so Kate became the decorator in general to the house, and the parlor gave evidence of her graceful fancies.

And yet, when John began seriously his study of chemistry, Kate was his sympathetic companion. She helped him often in making experiments when once his mother had fitted up his promised laboratory; and when, for recreation, those experiments took the form of photography, she helped him enthusiastically. Not a whit did she mind the stained fingers if she could flourish triumphantly a photograph of the house, taken by herself! Then, one after another, Molly and all her friends sat to the young artists, John attending to the camera and Kate to the posing and draping. Sometimes the order was reversed, and John posed the subjects and Kate

took the likeness; but there was always a good-
tempered outcry at this. Such dowdy dresses
as the women seemed to wear, with ramrods run
down them from crown to heel, and such enor-
mous hands! The men fared even worse.
They stood rigidly at "ease," and "lounged"
like wooden men. And so, at last, Kate was always the "artist" of the occasion.

Very soon John turned his attention to other
interesting things that his profession opened up
to him, but Kate only grew more fond of the
former pursuit; very soon she began to experiment and invent little improvements for herself, and her photographs gradually passed from
the first crude efforts to a softness and clear-
ness very like professional work; and some said
they had an individuality that the latter rarely
has.

Kate — who, of course, knew all about Meg's
love affair, and was an ardent admirer of Doctor
Milne — contrived to do her sister a great kindness at this time, and our tender little mother
winked at the proceeding. Of course, Kate did
not hide her light under a bushel (what genius
of fifteen ever does?), and the family portraits,
taken in every mood and manner, were sent
across the water; then those of their neighbors
and friends, and, of course, among them one of
Doctor Milne. I do not know whether Kate

thought that this would be very precious to Meg
or not, although I have no doubt she did; but
Molly knew, if Meg had not mistaken herself,
that this portrait would be very dear to her,
although she avoided seeming to think there was
any more significance in it than in sending that
of Mr. Lennox.

This taste of Kate's, and her apparent talent
for it, led Molly to wonder whether it might not
be a desirable career for her. True, she had
never heard of a woman photographer; but, a
few years ago, one never heard of a woman doctor; and, although a dozen physical reasons
might be urged against the latter profession for
women, she could not see one against photography. Before saying anything to Kate, or any
one else about it, Molly determined to consult
one of the best known New York photographers
about the matter. She did not know the artist
intimately, but she knew he would give her the
information.

Mr. Marani was an Italian, and he listened
courteously to what Molly told him, and evidently attached very little importance to what
she said about Kate's talent; even when she
showed what she considered Kate's best work,
he (after looking at it) only said : —

" Yes, there is evidence of artistic taste in the
posing, and even the photograph is very good
for an *amateur so young.*"

And Molly understood at once that he did not think it at all wonderful for an amateur of maturer age.

"Yes, it is quite good; but, to be candid, your daughter barely knows the A, B, C of the art, and there is the whole alphabet to learn. Who taught her so far?"

"No one. She has learned by experiment all she knows."

"Ah!" said Marani, taking up the photograph again. "That makes a difference. One who, with so little help, has taught herself so much may go far."

"But you don't think there is any reason why a woman should not make it a profession?"

"Certainly not. The best photographer in Naples is a woman! Only your daughter must not think the battle won, even after she has studied for years. I, to-day, feel that my art is but half learned, because new things are always turning up, and vast possibilities lie in the future, of which we get occasional glimpses, but cannot seize, although every artist worthy the name, all over the world, works to reach them every day and hour."

He gave her information as to what kinds of books to get, and where she might be able to obtain good instruction for Kate. For this he recommended a small Italian photographer, of no particular reputation.

" He knows, just as well as I do, all about the taking of photographs. He was my assistant, but he has no artistic taste; so he will never make a name — never, unless he finds some partner who is an artist. But he can teach all the mechanical part and the effects as well as any one, and your daughter will not need the artistic part; that can never be taught. If she has that in her, she will make a good artist; if she has it not, it is useless. She can take a likeness, but she could never make a good picture of it."

Molly left, feeling very hopeful. His manner had changed directly he found that Kate had worked unaided. Not to let the grass grow under her feet, and wishing to have some certain news to take home, she went to the address of Mr. Nelli, given her by Marani, and talked with him about her daughter. She found he was only too glad to have a pupil. He was married and evidently poor, and his wife, who lived on the premises (for he was not prospering enough to have a studio in a fashionable thoroughfare), acted as attendant.

Mrs. Nelli was a pretty and, seemingly, a very silly young American woman, who had, no doubt, been married for her *beaux yeux*, and brought nothing else to the housekeeping. The untidy, dusty little lounge, the carpet swept only in the centre, her own dress of faded pale blue, with shabby ribbons and dirty laces, showed that, without the glimpse Molly caught of a once trim little shoe, buttonless and untidy. Her head was apparently the seat of her vanity, and all the time she had for personal adornment was evidently bestowed on the arrangement of her hair.

Matters were soon settled between them, and when Molly reached home she had arranged for Kate to go into town daily to learn all she could with Mr. Nelli; and a year or two later she would try to give her further advantages, if her progress seemed to justify it.

CHAPTER XXV.

"ALL 'S WELL THAT ENDS WELL."

Time passes very swiftly to busy people, and much as Molly missed her dear companion, Meg, the year of her absence rolled rapidly away, and now the day of her return was at hand, and every one was busy in making the house look festive to welcome the travelers. Kate's taste and busy fingers, helped by generous gifts of flowers and smilax from Mary Lennox's now large green-houses, were to be depended on for the beautifying of the rooms, while Molly and John and Doctor Milne went to the steamer to meet them.

Molly smiled quietly to herself to see how entirely Doctor Milne considered himself one of the family; but she did not feel uneasy, for if every action of his had assured her he had not wavered in his affection, she could read between the lines of Meg's letters, and knew that distance and absence had but confirmed her affection for him. Reluctant as Molly had been to let them bind themselves, she was very happy to think George Milne was to be her son-in-law.

On looking back over her life, Molly was un-utterably grateful for the blessings she had en-joyed, and this marriage seemed the culmination of them all. She would have her daughter living near her, prosperous and happy, for she had not a doubt of Doctor Milne's ability to make any well-disposed woman so, and above all women, Meg.

A year in the "teens" works greater changes than at any other age in life, and although Meg's teens were almost over the change in her was very great. She looked prettier than ever, they all thought, as she flew to her mother the moment they stepped on deck, and had for a few seconds no eyes for any one but that dear, brave mother. John, on whose upper lip com-ing events were casting their shadows before, was at Molly's side, secretly hoping that he had grown out of knowledge, and that his mustache (he called the shadow by that name) would make him unrecognizable. Doctor Milne waited patiently in the background. His heart leaped and his eye brightened as, after her first loving impulse toward her mother, Meg looked swiftly round in search of some one even while she re-turned John's greeting. He had had time to take in the change in her, — the aroma of Eu-rope, as it were, that clung to her, — before he moved within her sight; then he caught the

vivid blush, the glad light that came to her eyes,
and knew that his hopes were not to be disappointed.

All the way out to Greenfield he had Meg
to himself. By some benign chance, the car
being pretty full, they had to take seats as they
could find them, and Meg and Doctor Milne
found theirs together. Mrs. Welles and Molly
were two seats before them, and Lois, John, and
Mr. Welles were at the other end.

A car is not a promising place to make love
in, especially if the lady is modest and the lover
not over bold ; but, notwithstanding the conditions, and although not an audible word had
been said, when they left the car they understood each other. Doctor Milne made this clear
to Molly by his triumphant eyes and the air of
possession which he unconsciously assumed.

"You see," said Mrs. Welles (she and Molly
went on, leaving the rest to see to the baggage),
"that my prophecy has come true."

"Yes, I see; I have not had much doubt of
it for some months, and I 'm thankful, oh, very
thankful ! "

"So am I ; Meg is the sweetest of women. I
always believed it ; now I have had her so long
under my wing I know it. But I must say I
think Doctor Milne is worthy of her."

When they reached the house it did, indeed,

wear a joyous air. The steps leading to the door had flowers on either side; the door was wreathed, and beside the flowers with which Kate had decorated every nook and corner, several of Mrs. Bishop's boarders, who almost always became her friends, had sent out beautiful baskets and boxes of rare fruit, flowers, and candies; all pleasing to Molly as a testimony to the affectionate respect in which she was held.

A dainty meal (neither dinner, nor tea, nor luncheon, since it was served at four) was ready for the travelers, who had been kept unusually long on the dock and were very ready to do justice to it; even the lovers made no pretense of not appreciating the good things before them.

There are few who have not enjoyed the merry reunion of loved ones who have been long parted, and this was perhaps no brighter than many another, although the room rang with happy laughter, and there were many stories told and many seemingly witty things said. The stories repeated would be flat, and the witty things poor trash to be told in cold blood. Wit, like poetry, often lies in the ear of him who hears it; and with these happy, joyous friends of ours a very little of the divine afflatus would go a long way.

But although happy reunions are known in most families, there is seldom a mother so overflowing with happiness as Molly Bishop. She has always been grateful to Providence for her good fortune, but in this last year all had turned out so well that she was made very humble. Why had every blessing been showered on her? She had had such a happy married life as few women know; then her children, they had always been so good that she was rather deprecating in her manner to other mothers whose offspring were often so different. It had almost seemed like exulting over them to speak of her own children's goodness. And then the prosperity of her business, — had many women, left as she was, been so favored by fortune?

Much of this she poured out from her full heart to her girlhood's friend, Charlotte Welles, when the two were closeted together that evening.

"I am almost frightened, Chatty. I've had such a prosperous life that I fear some calamity may be in store for me or mine. We are not meant to be so entirely happy in this world."

"That's just what we are meant to be, my dear, if our mean, discontented natures would allow us; but if you are uncomfortable and feel yourself too favored by fortune, we'll put it another way and see how it sounds. You were a bright young girl, with all a young girl's yearnings for pleasure; but you had a dear, half-in-

valid mother, who but for you must have had an
attendant, and as you had very small means,
that was not possible; so that, instead of the
usual pursuits of a girl of your age, you were already tied down with cares, studying hard in
order to meet the future, but, nevertheless, per-
forming all the duties of nurse together with the
hundred things a daughter would do and an attendant would not.   Now, this is not the picture
of a gay and giddy girlhood " —

"No," interrupted Molly, smiling; "but it was
a very happy one.   No one ever had a happier
girlhood than I."

" Yes, *you* were very happy ; you did not fret
over the constant self-repression.   I don't suppose you were conscious of it, but I would like
to know how many girls would have been more
than dutifully content, and would not have en-
vied the freedom and pleasures of other girls,
from behind the bars of their cage, — in other
words, the windows of the sick-room.

" Your next great cause of happiness (after
your poor mother's death, and the loss of income
which you had always been prepared for) came
in your going out as governess and finding a tol-
erable position."

" Oh, a very comfortable one ! "

" Nevertheless, several governesses had left
at the end of three months, and you can't deny

that it took all the time you had to fill the duties required."

" I know; but they were all so kind to me.   I was alone in this country although born here, but they made me one of themselves."

" Yes, but they got more out of you than a governess ever gives.   Why, you actually used to trim Mrs. Plummer's bonnets, write her letters, go shopping," —

" Ah, but you forget; I was never asked to do anything outside of my duties.   The rest was doing myself a pleasure."

" I know, dear, I know all about it," said Mrs. Welles, her eyes resting with tender affection on Molly.

" Well, then you married the most beautiful young man."   Mrs. Welles's voice softened as she came to the tender spot in Molly's memory. "And there, I do think, you had cause for happiness.   Dear Harry was a sweet fellow; but every woman who marries the man she loves thinks that, although most of them would have allowed the treatment of his family to mar the perfection of their lives.   The outward circumstances of your marriage were not brilliant; you had to work hard for all your pleasure. Look at me; I have been a fairly happy and fortunate woman.   I did nothing to deserve the easy and luxurious life I have led since my

marriage. But I confess I am not overpowered
by a sense of my own unworthiness, nor do I
dread a calamity in consequence. Then, dear,
this great happiness ended so soon that because
it was so great you might well consider your
loss misfortune enough to counterbalance all
great blessings since. But you were of different
stuff; you did not make a moan over the cruelty
of fate, although *we* all thought it was cruel for
you. Then the position of a young widow, with
two young children and posthumous baby, does
not seem to me a very fortunate one, nor the life
of hard work and unflagging duty you have led
since.

"In fact, dear Molly, I think to most women
the story would seem a piteous one of a very
hard life, full of troubles. The happiness of it
has been in *you*, dear, who have never looked
out for the woe, the struggles, and hardships in
it, but only for its blessings. Above all, you
have never taken to *pitying yourself.* Instead
of comparing yourself with people less deserving
but better off (me, for example, who, though
I 'm good-natured, never have been called upon
for self-denial), and wondering why you should
struggle and they not, as most of us do, you have
compared yourself with the less well off, and
been grateful.

" I could almost preach a sermon on your life, Molly, and the text would be, ' Work hard without thinking it hard, and that " will-o'-the-wisp " perfect happiness will come without seeking. If ever a woman reaped the harvest she has sowed, that woman is Molly Bishop ! ' "

Molly's eyes were brimming, her lips quivered at this true friend's words. They loved each other well, although they did not often say much about it. It was sweet to find Charlotte thought so well of her, but even that seemed only another instance of her good fortune ; she had even more and better friends than most people.

. . . .

The story of Molly Bishop's struggles is told. The calamity she feared when her cup seemed overflowing has not overtaken her yet. May it never be more than the shadow thrown by the sun of happiness.

Meg lives in a beautiful home near ¬her mother, and is as happy as can be.

John, who believes he is destined to do great things in the way of chemical discovery (and what is more others think so too), is very constantly with Lois ; and Molly and Mrs. Welles have a pleasant conviction that their friendship will be cemented by a marriage between the two families.

Kate vows she will never marry, but will stay with her mother and devote herself to her profession. But Kate is very young yet, and such resolutions are frequent with very young women.

THE END.